5-16

When she turned from Frank to begin the trip back to the car, she stopped short. There was a haze of some sort, a fog-like substance swirling in the air a short distance before her. As she stared, the haze grew denser, and she thought she could make out shapes within it. Her eyes must have been playing tricks, she reasoned, so she rubbed them with both hands and then looked back. In the few seconds it took to rub the disbelief from her eyes, the shapes had taken ghostly but distinct forms. Claudine gasped.

Before her stood the shades of ten men in service uniforms, their visage like waves of heat rising from a sun-burnt blacktop. They were smiling, wholly formed, and walking toward her husband's gravesite in formation. When they arrived, they broke rank and formed a broad circle around the grave. They stood there, rigid and unmoving, all of them gazing at the flat stone. As if a silent signal had been transmitted, they all went to their knees, and in unison, ten hands reached down and disappeared into the dirt. When their hands withdrew moments later, an eleventh hand could be seen floating up through the ground, clinging tightly to the others. They pulled Claudine's husband up, and he now stood with the ten, grinning and looking as handsome as he ever had. The ten welcomed him as only brothers could.

To: Griffin Free Library
+ 1. for the support!

D1235709

V (14)

This book is dedicated to Nancy Kalanta

CONTENTS

SIFTING THROUGH
THE SEEDS OF NIGHTMARES
AN INTRODUCTION BY JOHN MCILVEEN

I have a confession. I'm not usually a fan of short stories. I know it seems blasphemous coming from a writer of many short stories, but I often find myself feeling shortchanged after reading them. I come away either wondering where the hell the rest of the story is, feeling grossed out, or completely mind-numbed by some present-day philosopher who has a cryptic vision only a PhD could decipher.

With short stories, an author is given a window—usually 7500 words or less—through which they can offer their wares, and in *Horror*, it seems to me that too many authors squander this word limit trying to send you reeling and running for a barf bag, a therapist, or a thesaurus.

It is not this way with Tony. I love his stories.

Like a toboggan ride down an unfamiliar, twisting slope, they're fast, slick, a whole lot of fun, and what I like most (a smooth salve to one of my greatest pet peeves with stories—short or long) is they have a decisive ending. Oh, Tony may fool you and send you careening into a brick wall or over a cliff, but you'll get up, shake it off, and head back up that slope hankering for the next ride.

In *The Seeds of Nightmares*, Tony offers us a smorgasbord – a feast of emotions and genres that cover the spectrum. Take his opening offering for example, the nasty little novelette "The Strange Saga of Mattie Dyer," a darkly humorous, Lovecraftian, western tale of vengeance (yes, you read that right). The story is wrought with unsavory and despicable characters—a thwarted woman, a vile creature, redneck gold-diggers, and Indians—it's a virtual Pandora's Box and a hell of a first run. Look out for the holes!

In "Something New," (my favorite) a thwarted husband bent on revenge finds himself snared in a deadly blizzard he can only escape by acknowledging the sins of his past. Vengeance (a consistent, well-handled theme in many of Tony's stories) takes a surprising turn in "The Black Dress," where it's a jilted lover versus his cheating wife. Who will win? I guess it all comes down to perspective. In the little noir gem "The Old Man," an ex-mobster finds that hiding from his kingpin isn't as easy as he hoped, and in "The Soldier's Wife," a widow confronts the truth of her boorish deceased husband's past while attending his funeral.

A few of these tales may make you uncomfortable, like "An Alabama Christmas," which might be the most disturbing Christmas Story you will ever read, and "Stardust," which gives us a twisted celestial tale of redemption, retaliation, and hope within an unusual family—presented in a way quite unlike any Joni Mitchell might have envisioned.

Tony takes aim at family in "The Burial Board", as a man's attempt to fulfill his grieving wife's appeal goes horribly wrong. Tony again targets family, but goes for the heart in "Tsunami," a part-mystical, part-existential tale of woman who survives the tsunami that claims her family during a tropical vacation, only to find that it is the doorway to truth (if she so chooses)…or is it? It continues with "Husband of Kellie," where a wife is driven to do the unthinkable, which only gets worse from there. In "The Pawnshop," a man is forced into a Catch-22 that threatens the lives of his wife and daughter, and "The Visitors," is a corkscrew of a tale about a campground owner who encounters a mother and daughter team who rock her like a hurricane.

Perfectly placed about halfway through, Tony balances the collection—but knocks us dizzy—with "Chiyoung and Dongsun's Song," a hilarious and unusual allegory tale of Korean yore about an unusual young man whose affections for an unusual young woman drives him to unusual lengths to make himself irresistible to her through unusual means. Did I say it was unusual?

As with the best story collections and anthologies, *The Seeds of Nightmares* is a wonderful blending of genres, sentiments, and sensations, and like Tony himself, is chuck-full-o-heart (Yes, those who know Tony are aware of his penchant for cute animal videos and misty-eyed Facebook posts). There will be twists, bumps, a little blood, and possibly a few tears, but you're tough...you can take it.

So have a seat, strap in, and enjoy the ride!

—John McIlveen
Haverhill, Massachusetts
January 4th, 2016

I've always had a fascination with holes. My obsession started back in 1991 with a reading of The Cipher by Kathe Koja, a novel about a young woman who discovers a black hole on the floor of a nearby apartment. The Cipher was unrelenting—it was bleak, gritty, and creepy as hell. As much as I enjoyed it, I thought it lacking in one element that would have made it perfect—more black humor. For two decades I kicked the concept around on how to make a story with a hole as a plot point terrifying, yet make it bizarre enough to leave a reader with a smile at the tale's end.

I attempted two short stories, "Holes" (which was published in The Writers Den at Horror World), and "Stanley's Hole" (which was published in Dark Eclipse Digest). Both were fun, but I wanted to do something longer and more involved with the concept.

A few years ago, I reviewed a weird western novel by Steven Savile and David Niall Wilson called Hallowed Ground. I loved the story, and the notion of combining supernatural elements with an Old West theme appealed to me. I decided to try my hand at writing a weird western using a supernatural hole as the plot device and "The Strange Saga of Mattie Dyer" was born. Several first readers, including my writers group, Janet Holden, Thad Linson, David Dodd, and Keith Minnion read the first draft of the story. Their encouragement spurred me on.

The original novella was 50,000 words, but after removing two-thirds of it (the portion of the story takes place after "The Strange Saga of Mattie Dyer" ends), I was ready to submit it for this collection. Before I got the chance to send it to Crossroad Press, John McIlveen asked if he could read the story. John came back with some line edits, and a suggestion I add a prologue, which would result in a tightening of the dialog later in story. When I asked John why he went out of his way for me, he explained Rick Hautala had once done the same for him, and John was simply passing it on. Because of people like John and Rick, I often reflect on how fortunate I am to be involved in this genre.

The Strange Saga of Mattie Dyer

Prologue

Three brothers focused on the solitary cow in the corral, their eyes gleaming in the waning light of the sun. Clothed only in loincloths, they sat cross-legged with their hands clasped and resting on their laps. Their testicles, sticky and raw from the day's heat, nestled in the desert sand as dusk delivered its requisite chill to the valley. The Indians were scouting the only remaining farm in the valley.

A young man, scrawnier than a Joshua tree, and who possessed as much sense, lived in the cabin on the farm. His mate, a timid woman who rarely ventured outside, had even less meat on her bones. This couple promised the least resistance to their poaching, so the brothers saved their farm for last.

With the light of the full moon to guide them, the brothers stooped and ran the distance to the corral. Slipping through the gaps in the fence, they crept toward the cow. The oldest of the brothers slowed, reached down to his thigh and slipped a knife from its sheath. The other two, reaching the animal first, steadied its head until the eldest caught up. He placed the tip of his blade against the animal's throat, and mumbled a prayer of thanks to the Old Ones. When he finished the devotion, he plunged the knife into the animal's throat and then twisted it, slicing through muscle and gristle to enlarge the wound. The cow bucked in fear as the three brothers stood back and waited for their dinner to bleed out. When their meal collapsed to the ground, they gutted it.

It was the brothers' turn to hunt the Whites' food—to take what they needed, when they needed it. The Whites had come in droves, setting up villages and digging in the mountains for gold rock.

They killed any game they came upon, far more than they could eat, and sometimes they hunted and killed merely for sport. The Indians often came upon food left to rot where it lay. Hungry and desperate, they consumed the decaying game.

Their plan this evening had been to gather as much meat as possible from the animal, and then return with it to their encampment. Their father would appreciate the bounty, and they would all eat well for many days. They knew when these Whites left, as all the other Whites in the valley had, food would once again be scarce, but that was a problem for another day.

As they cleaned the animal, their plans changed.

The cabin door swung open, and the brothers turned toward it. The white man pushed his way through the opening and climbed down the porch stairs, singing and pretending to strum a guitar, unaware of them as he made his way to the outhouse. He stopped midway to the structure, lifted his head, and sniffed the air. The brothers knew what he smelled. They bathed in it. The White turned toward the corral, and even from this distance they could see his eyes widen. The White's surprise turned into fury.

They were not concerned. They were ready for him.

The White charged toward a short-handled ax leaning against a water pump, reached out and grabbed it, never breaking stride. He lifted his weapon high, slashing the air in frantic arcs as he ran toward the Indians.

The eldest looked to his brothers, grinned, nodded, and then stepped into the White's path as the others stepped back and off to the side. The White continued on, spittle flying from his mouth as he swung the ax from left to right. He charged the eldest brother who made a beckoning motion with his fingers. The other two flanked the White, both holding tightly to their knives.

When the White reached the elder brother, he paused, raised the ax behind his head and over his shoulder blades, inhaled deeply, and then lunged. The two brothers came up from behind and stuck their blades deep into his stomach.

The White's eyes went wide and the ax's descent stopped above his head, and then it fell from his hands. Shoulders slumped and head bowed, he fell to his knees, his hands slipping to his wounds in a futile attempt to stop the bleeding. When he tried to stand, the

Indians slashed their knives in a flurry, each thrust sinking deep into the White's back. Their frustration and hate boiled—an entire village would not have had enough hands to cover the wounds they made. When their energy ebbed, the Indians kicked the White over, laughing as he groaned. The White spoke one last word as he died. With blood bubbling from his lips, he whispered, "Mattie."

Only the elder brother understood what the White had said. He turned his head toward the cabin, and the others followed his gaze. Though the woman could not have heard her mate call, she heard the commotion. The door to the cabin opened and she stood on the porch, her eyes scanning the landscape and then focusing on the structure where they shit. "John?" she called. "John?"

With another nod from the eldest, the three brothers turned their attentions to Mattie.

CHAPTER ONE

Southwestern Utah
June 22, 1880

Mattie Dyer's soul was empty.

The most one might expect from Mattie in response to a "howdy, Miss" or a "good day, Ma'am" would be a non-committal shrug or, in the worst case, a lingering stare so fierce it could set one's hair on fire. Why all that hostility and indifference? It was her way of holding up a sign, no different from the ones hanging on the front of the gunsmith's shop or the general store. It was Mattie's way of telling others that at one time or another she had been a victim—something she did not ever intend to be again.

To Mattie, a smile possessed no more relevance than a frown. If she deigned to show one or the other, a person would have to look closely past the lines and wrinkles on her sun-bleached face to tell the difference. She had lived a tough life, experiencing more pain and sorrow than any female character in those cowboy-themed dime novels she devoured in her youth. And like a young girl tugging on her mama's dress, troubles were never too far behind Mattie Dyer.

It was less than six months after they had moved to Utah when her husband had been taken from her. After his passing, the weeks alone on the farm had stretched into months, and then years, giving Mattie plenty of time to crawl into herself and shut out the world. It had never occurred to Mattie that she had changed since her husband was murdered, that she might have become peculiar or unusual. She was what she was, a survivor who cared little about how she was perceived by others.

But at that moment, if someone had stood on the dusty patch of ground adjacent to her collapsed barn and gazed her way, they would have seen an almost imperceptible look of concern in her countenance as she pumped away at her well on a rust-worn jack handle. Mattie was feeling uneasy, something she had not experienced in quite a spell.

Normally Mattie approached unusual events similarly, cataloguing them in her memory and then filing them away alongside the other minutiae of her workday. She gave little thought to either the gifts or the travails that God had sent her way, but at this point in her life, this feeling of uneasiness was foreign to her and it demanded attention. She let go of the jack handle, straightened her back, and took a cautious look around the ranch.

She ignored the distressed state of her cabin and its surroundings; her eyes swept the dry and dusty ground instead, taking note of the fowl that roamed in front of her cabin, the pigs in their sty and, finally, the lone horse lined up at the trough in the corral. While they all appeared to be safe and accounted for, they, too, seemed on edge, unnaturally quiet and crowding close to their own. Something wasn't right and she was damned if she could figure it out.

Mattie had an overwhelming feeling of being watched and, out of character, she felt vulnerable.

Instinct kicked in. She glanced around, her eyes scouring the ground for a weapon and spied a small, short-handled ax nestled into a pile of leaky buckets that she had discarded over the years. Walking the few yards separating her from the weapon, she reached down and lifted it. She wiped its head against her dress, cleaning it as best she could for further inspection. A quick run of her fingers over its edge revealed some blunting, but she thought it still sharp enough to cleave brush. Maybe bone, if it came to that.

Her thoughts of the ax were interrupted when a chill, akin to ice pressing against her spine, made her shudder. There was nothing in her line of sight that would cause this feeling but something in her peripheral vision caught her attention. She raised the ax into striking position.

Mattie didn't gasp, shriek, or do more than raise an eye when she spotted the source of her unnerving. Off to her side, close to fifteen feet away, an odd object lay on the ground. It was flat and circular, about three feet in diameter and so dark she took its color to be black.

Lowering the ax, Mattie advanced toward it.

Her first thought was that it was a piece of wood painted black, perhaps a cover for a barrel or a loose piece of planking that had fallen off of a passing wagon. She realized it was neither of those things. It occurred to her that it could be a hole, though she could see no depth to it. Its darkness was absolute; she could see no further than past its surface. Mattie stood close at its edge and shivered again. Her feeling of being observed intensified, and she stepped back.

Mattie lowered herself on bended knees until she was low to the ground. She reached out, gathered a few stones with her free hand, and then rose. She hesitated for a moment, and then tossed the stones onto the object.

They bounced off, landing harmlessly in the dirt.

Mattie's discomfort did not abate for there was no sound when the stones struck the surface.

Stepping closer, leaving less than a foot between her and whatever that thing was, she kneeled before it and scrutinized its surface. Whatever this object was, it was not natural. Despite her misgivings, she could not leave it alone. She placed the ax on the ground by her side, yet clung to its handle for assurance. She brought her free hand up and held it inches above the object, and then lowered her fingers until their tips touched its surface.

Mattie was unprepared for the sensation.

She had expected to feel some type of resistance, something hard, metallic maybe, perhaps static electricity. Instead, it felt damp, soft, warm, and slippery, although her fingers remained dry.

It might have been curiosity or confusion, or the object itself calling out to her somehow, but Mattie was compelled to press her fingertips into the surface.

They sank into the blackness.

She withdrew her hand in panic, turning it left and right, looking for damage. She exhaled a noisy puff of breath in relief when she determined it had not been affected.

She stared at the object, thinking of it as more of a hole than something solid. A hole, she mused, that seemed to allow only fingers, not rocks into it. She wondered if only living objects that were permitted through its surface. Mattie looked about to see if any of her chickens were nearby. They were always about pecking in the dirt, but it seemed as if they were staying far away from the hole. Instead of taking a lesson from her hens, she decided to experiment further.

Opening her hand, she splayed her fingers, placed them palm down onto the surface, and pressed. As her hand descended, the feeling of dampness returned. It wasn't an unpleasant feeling, just an odd one. She moved her hand slightly back and forth, wondering if she would feel any resistance.

The hole seemed empty.

Mattie moved her hand toward the side, her eyes widened when her hand traveled past the point where it should have touched.

She leaned forward, placing more weight on the hand that held the ax and lowered her arm into the hole until it was almost up to her elbow.

She felt something slight, almost like a tickle that traveled up and down the length of her arm. It reminded her of the time when she was a kid and went fishing with her dad. While he fished, she stuck her arm into the pond and hundreds of tiny minnows swam up to nibble at her. At the time, she had imagined the minnows were kissing her, and that's what this felt like—little fish kisses.

Intrigued, she rotated her arm in a circular pattern to see if the nibbling sensation followed. When it did, she smiled. She decided that she should lower her arm into the hole to see if she could touch bottom. As her arm descended, the tickling sensation ceased. Surprised, she cocked her head and lowered it closer to the hole.

Something coiled around her arm and tightened.

As sharp as barbed wire, it sunk deeply into her skin. Mattie cried out as she tried to lift her arm, but whatever had her held tight. She stopped struggling, hoping the pause would give her time to think, but she didn't have the chance. Pain spread up her arm like wildfire as fishhooks tunneled under her skin. She felt them crawl, like ants descending on scraps of meat. Their motion turned feverous, her flesh and muscles igniting in agony as it chewed her arm from the inside out.

Mattie was no stranger to pain. In her lifetime, she had shed plenty of tears due to its influence, but if you compared all those wails and screams from her past they wouldn't come close to the intensity of the shrieks now emanating from her throat. She screamed until her vocal cords were raw, and blood mixed with spit clung to her chin. She pulled and pulled, trying to lift her arm out of the hole, but it was to no avail. She was exhausted, on the verge of passing out and falling into the hole.

Then, the pain vanished.

Slumped over, with her arm still dangling in the hole, Mattie rested. Though physically drained, she took a deep breath and prepared for another attempt at escape. She felt a tug on her shoulder, and then another. She grimaced as her arm rotated, and then there was another tug on her shoulder. She tried to pull her arm free as another tug, so violent that it set her chin flying upward, set the nerves in her neck on fire. The next tug came seconds later, nearly strong enough to pull her into the hole, but she jammed her free arm into the ground, stopping her momentum. She closed her eyes in thanks to a god she never believed in, but a movement below her caused them to snap back open. Her arm started bobbing in the hole. The pace was slow, like a leaf caught on a pond's ripple, but it quickened and was soon thrashing like a fish out of water. Desperate not to fall, she leaned back, surprised when her arm followed, though it remained submerged. She kneeled astride the hole, her calves straining as her arm danced a macabre jig.

Then, the thrashing of her arm stopped.

Minutes passed as she stared into the hole. A silence hung in the air and a surreal calm overtook her. Mattie had been mistaken when she first lowered her hand into the hole. Those weren't minnows tickling her arm earlier. They were sharks.

Mattie lifted herself into a crouching position, balanced her weight on the upper soles of her feet, and pushed with her legs. Daggers dug into her lower back and she screamed, but her arm held tight. She imagined it tearing off at the shoulder if she continued. She was reaching her pain limit, and she thought the battle lost. With one final hope, she closed her eyes, clenched her teeth, and with a feral scream, she pushed with her remaining strength.

The next thing she knew, she was staring at the sky.

The hole had given up its claim on her, and she had tumbled backward, landing flat on her back. She took a few seconds to collect herself instead of rising quickly. When her breathing evened and the soreness in her back eased, Mattie looked at her arm.

There was a monster attached to it.

It was florescent green, with small silver-dollar-sized, ivory-colored discs lined in neat rows up and down its length. Where her fingers should have been were five long tentacles that danced wildly in the air. At the tip of each tentacle were triangle-shaped orifices that reminded Mattie of lips. The triangles opened and closed like baby birds crying for worms. When they opened, she could see more triangles resembling teeth, bone white and razor sharp.

As the tentacles flailed through the air, she realized that their motions were not random or born from confusion; they had purpose, as if they were searching.

One swung in Mattie's direction, locked on her, and froze. Seconds later, they all turned toward her, lined themselves in a row, and then hovered in place, standing tall, sleek, and erect. Although they were barely as wide as one of her dinner knives, and maybe twice the length, she couldn't help wondering if they were as strong as the steel used to make those knives.

Mattie's gaze traveled along the length of her arm. She had never seen anything this horrible looking. She saw no seam where the hellish monster had attached itself to her; it looked as if the damned thing had swallowed her arm whole. Though she felt no pain, that didn't mean she wouldn't if she tried to take it off her arm.

She returned her focus to the tentacles. They were appraising her, staring her down, but she was perplexed as to how as they didn't have anything that resembled eyes. She could only stare back, knowing that if this were a challenge of some sort, she would be the loser.

It was then that Mattie remembered the ax. Without taking her gaze away from the monster, she squeezed her hand tight around the handle.

The opportunity to use it came quickly.

The tentacles went rigid, upright and unwavering—their lips open to their fullest. It was time to act.

Mattie's time ran out when the monster struck first.

All five tentacles dove toward her with blinding speed, clamping down on her skirt-covered thigh, and pinning her to the ground.

They began to feast.

Mattie screamed, the sounds escaping from her throat were low and guttural, a harrowing mixture of torment and fright.

Mattie raised her upper body to see if she could do anything to remove it, but her despair worsened upon seeing the small chunks of her flesh, bloody and stringy, clinging to her skirt and falling to the dirt as the lips chewed. If she didn't stop them soon, they would eat down to the bone.

Mattie sat up and raised the ax, facing the blunt end toward the monster. With a yell so loud the tentacles paused from their feasting, she brought the ax down against the body of the monster, sinking it deep. Fluid as yellow as cow's piss sprayed out in thin streams in all directions. The monster jerked madly, and Mattie's shoulder convulsed as the tentacles detached from her thigh. They swung around to the injury and hovered above it.

Mattie drew her hand back, preparing for another blow, but paused. Something wasn't right. She should have felt that blow. Wasn't her arm inside the monster?

It dawned on her—the monster hadn't simply attached itself to her arm. Instead, the damn thing had taken its place. It had grown, and it was now attached to her above the elbow.

How long would it take for it to consume the rest of me?

She didn't wait to find out. Maneuvering herself onto her knees, Mattie took what she hoped would be her last good look at it. She raised the ax high and took aim at where its body had merged with her own.

The blade easily cleaved through its body. Mattie hadn't felt so much as a tickle when it separated from her arm and fell to the ground.

The monster writhed on the sand.

Mattie thought that its thrashing was due to anger, not feelings of pain or confusion. Yellow liquid spewed from its severed end, staining the ground in random, swirling patterns. The tentacles had simply wilted after the amputation, draping themselves over the monster like dying lovers.

It convulsed for no more than half a minute before abruptly ceasing, its yellow blood slowing to a dribble. Mattie thought it dead, but taking no chances, she backed away from it. She should have been relieved that her fight was over, but something came to her as she stood there watching its death throes. She hadn't seen any of her own blood, and she felt no pain in her stump.

She released her grip on the ax, dropping it noiselessly to the sand where it came to rest against the monster's body. With her remaining hand, she grabbed at the shoulder of her severed arm, holding it steady so she could view it.

She looked up to the heavens, her face tightening, and when the sky began to spin, she closed her eyes to keep from getting sick.

Mattie had expected to see sliced muscle and exposed bone, but the stub of her forearm had already healed. The flesh covering the wound was florescent green and at its center was an ivory-colored disc about the size of a silver dollar.

She tried to fight off the dizziness enveloping her, but exhausted, she willingly ceded the battle, lost consciousness and collapsed.

Falling backward, she hit the ground hard and broke two vertebrae in her back. Her skull, however, was spared any type of injury.

The back of Mattie's head had landed in the hole.

CHAPTER TWO

June 23, 1880

Much of the western portion of Utah is made up of sand, and in its southwest corner lies a small portion of one of the largest deserts in the country—the Mojave. It was here where a pair of cowboys rode through parched, hard-packed sand on their way to Spring Valley, California.

It was early in the day, and whatever deity controlled the sun this morning had cranked it up to broil. Heat waves danced upon the distant sand, shimmering and then rising into the dead dry air. No matter which direction they looked, the view would have been distorted, unfocused, and no amount of squinting would have made it any clearer. To be out in this heat was foolish for most living things, as the men were painfully aware.

The scorching heat was a sharp contrast to the bone-chilling cold they had endured when traveling over the Colorado Rockies, but as uncomfortable as they were, the two had no intention of turning around. They had come from the East, having left Kansas weeks earlier with the dream of striking it rich.

The word back in Kansas was that there was gold in California and, from the talk in the banks and saloons, there was plenty enough in the hills for everyone willing to work for it. It wouldn't be easy, but hard work didn't bother them: like eating, breathing, and aging—it came naturally.

They weren't young. Their shoulders sagged from the weight of their years, and their muscles, though well developed from decades on the cattle trails, ached from thirty plus years of sleeping on the ground and from their asses hugging a saddle. Nobody could blame them for wanting a better life, and certainly none of the cattle bosses did. There was no real money in being a cowpoke. Other than a roof over his head and three squares, there wasn't much else a cowboy could count on when he was on the trail. While the work was honest and the pay fair, there was little left after all the whoring, drinking, and gambling between drives.

The cowboys had been riding through the desert in the cool moonlight and continued on further in the early morning hours. As late morning approached, they were ready to make camp, get some sleep, and then wait out the rest of the blistering day. They spied some hazy rock formations that appeared tall enough to shade them and their horses. They trotted toward the shelter and dismounted, intending to walk their horses the short distance to the shady side of the outcropping. Turning the corner, they stopped when they encountered an old man.

His face was scruffy and pitted as the ragged rocks against which he leaned, his clothes well worn, stained and loose fitting. Tethered to a Joshua tree several feet to his left was a horse with a saggy gut, pawing at the dusty ground. The old man's saddle, which had also seen better days, was on the dirt, close to the horse. A rucksack was laid out in front of the old-timer, its meager contents scattered about.

"Howdy, gentlemen," greeted the old-timer, offering a widely spaced brown-toothed smile.

He looked harmless enough, but they had run into strangers on the trail who'd offer to share a drink and then try to slit their throats for the money in their pockets. Their first inclination was to grab their side arms, and the shorter of the two men lowered his right hand to his Colt, but neither of them drew their guns.

"Howdy back at ya," the taller of the two men replied.

The old man stood, hitched his pants, and extended a dirt-encrusted hand. "Name's Walter," he said, "and yer welcome to share my rock. It's hotter 'n a roasting pit out there and you two look to be well done enough. Come on, git in the shade."

The taller cowboy relaxed and extended his hand. "My name's Roy," he offered. Pointing to his companion, he said, "This here's Chuck."

"Well, boys, pleased to meet ya. Let me guess, yer headed to California to dig up some of that gold?" asked Walter as they shook hands. The reek hit them immediately, the old man smelled as bad as he looked.

Roy and Chuck nodded in agreement.

"Thought so. Don't see many men on this trail, but when I do, that's where they's headed. Hope you boys are good friends. I've seen lots of misery come to men whether they find gold or don't. It surely will test a friendship."

"We've rode together but only recently. I figure we know each other enough so we have each other's back," said Chuck, eyeing the man hard, implying that the old man had better not try anything. The old man chuckled.

The two cowboys unsaddled their horses and tied them alongside the old man's horse. They rummaged through their packs for food, grabbed their canteens, and sat on either side of the old man, their backs leaning against the rock wall. The two men offered Walter some jerky, which he readily accepted. Roy then held out his canteen.

"No thanks, young fella," Walter mumbled, his mouth full of jerky. "Got enough to make it to the Rockies, but from the looks of those water bags on yer horses, seems like you two are gonna need all you can git. Where you fellas headed?"

"Spring Valley," Roy replied. "We figure it's about a two-day ride from here."

"Well, yer close—more like three. If you could ride during the day, you might make it in two, but there ain't no way in this heat. You'd use up quite a bit of water on them horses, never mind between the two of ya's."

A look of concern passed between Roy and Chuck. They had filled their canteens and water bags in the mountains, thinking they'd reach Spring Valley before running out. A day wouldn't make much of a difference to them. They could ration their water, but the heat was brutal and their worry was for the horses.

"Don't be lookin' all that glum, fellas; there's a place 'bout a day and a half out from Spring Valley. Ain't much of a spread, but if you can git her old pump to work, ya can fill up. You'll be fine if you make it to Mattie's."

Chuck's interest was piqued at the mention of a woman's name. "Mattie's?"

"Yeah, she owns the spread. If ya got somethin' to trade for the water, she'll take it, but if not, she'll let ya git your fill. Either way, just be off when yer done."

Chuck let this churn in his head for a few seconds and then asked, "Just be off when you're done? What's her story? She got a man?"

Walter's eyes turned hard. "First off, she ain't got no man no more. I don't reckon she needs one as she's done all right for herself this last year or so, and I'll tell ya right now, son, you'll be sorry if ya mess with her. As for her story, well, it's a long one, and it ain't a good one."

"We got time," Roy replied between chews of jerky.

The old man straightened his back and wiggled his rump in an effort to get comfortable and then began.

"Mattie's story made all the papers. Sherriff even got one of 'em Injun boys involved to tell what happened. T'was all anyone 'round here talked 'bout for months. Men still talk 'bout it in the taverns, wimmen', too, in their own circles, I'd guess.

"Mattie and her husband came to Spring Valley in seventy-eight. Brigham Young sent a bunch of them Mormons down that way to claim whatever land they could so his reach could expand below Salt Lake. Gave 'em all a grubstake and told 'em to be fruitful and to multiply. Six couples made their way down and helped each other build small ranches. Didn't take too long 'fore they all had a hard time of it, though. That land don't take to farmin' much. They spent more money in Spring Valley buyin' food and supplies than they'd planned. The livestock did okay fer the most part. They survived the heat and there was plenty of scrub fer the horses, but the cattle and chickens needed feed, and like I said, they spent more money on it than they'd planned. But that's not what drove most of 'em out in the end. 'Twas the Injuns."

At the mention of Indians, Roy's eyebrows lifted, but he didn't say anything.

"'Bout six months 'fore Mattie and her bunch showed up, the weather here was the worst I can 'member, and I've lived round here fer most of my life. There weren't a whole lot of snow in the mountains that winter, but the cold was brutal. Then spring decided to skip us altogether and the summer heat came early. It burned up the land, left it barren. While nature was shittin' on us, the miners were also doing their damnedest to destroy the area by headin' up to the mountains and huntin' anythin' they could. They took deer, rabbit, elk, and mountain sheep—hell, anythin' with four legs that stepped into their gun sights. And the Injuns, well, they didn't take too kindly to it."

"I thought the Indians had all signed treaties and were placed on reservations or farms," Roy said, confused. He had asked about Indian activity around the mines before agreeing to take the trip west with Chuck and he was told there was nothing to be concerned about.

Walter nodded. "Most were. One tribe north of here, the Go-shutes, lived mostly in the desert, close to the mountains and in small clans. The miners and the Mormons came and pushed 'em out, and then the gov'ment sent most of them to farms and reservations, but a few went south. One of those clans, headed up by a chief called Long Elk and his three sons, settled 'round here. With the bad weather and the nearby mountains 'bout hunted out, those Injuns were angry and hungry.

"Long Elk's boys 'ventually raided all the Mormon spreads, leavin' Mattie's fer last, maybe 'cause it was closest to Spring Valley. Livin' in fear of more raids and with almost no livestock left, those Mormons went back to Salt Lake, leavin' Mattie and her husband behind. Mattie was a timid woman back then, havin' little choice but to stay with her man who insisted he weren't leavin'. Thought God had spared them from the worst, I imagine. Turned out God must have been busy makin' that magical underwear for Brigham Young. Seems He forgot all about poor Mattie and her husband."

Chuck looked over to Roy. "Magical underwear?"

Roy shook his head. "I'll explain it to you later. Got something to do with their religion. Go ahead, Walter, let's hear the rest."

The old man chuckled at Chuck's ignorance, but his face remained set.

"Long Elk's boys came to Mattie's spread 'bout a week after the rest of 'em Mormons pulled up stakes. Was near dusk, and those Injuns was as quiet as a cat stalkin' a dove. They snuck into the pen and killed Mattie's cow, slit its throat and then gutted it. Mattie's husband, John, spotted 'em in the pen when he went to use the privy.

"John was as stupid as he was stubburn. Instead of runnin' back to the cabin and grabbin' a gun, he charged those Injuns with a small ax that was lyin' by the pump.

"Now, Long Elk weren't only a chief, he was a medicine man. Rumor was he could conjure up some bad spirits, even monsters from whatever hell those Injuns believed in. Anyways, he fed those Injun boys roots, herbs, and the such to keep 'em healthy enough to provide fer the four of 'em. Those boys mighta been hungry, but they were strong, and ole John, who was on the scrawny side, well, he didn't stand a chance against 'em."

Roy spoke just barely above a whisper. "They killed him."

The old man shook his head. "Worse, they played with him first."

"Did, did they scalp him?" asked Roy, visibly shaking.

"The Go-shutes don't scalp their victims. They took their knives and opened up his belly. John's guts spilt over the ground, and they left him there to suffer. When Spring Valley's sheriff and deputy came they couldn't tell whose insides they were lookin' at—John's or the cow's."

Roy swallowed hard. Walter didn't need to provide further detail of what happened to John, as Roy's imagination did it all on its own. Since Roy was a child, Indians had haunted his nightmares. When they occupied his thoughts while he was on the trails, he used every trick he had to banish them. Sometime he was successful, but more often than not, images of the Indians' savagery would return.

When Roy was young, his father would gather the family together after dinner and read aloud from the weeklies or from dime novels. Roy and his brother would sit and listen on the rug, usually playing board games like Around the World or checkers, while their mother would knit in her rocking chair. His father would take particular delight when reciting the passages concerning the atrocities the Indians committed, often emphasizing the more gruesome ones. The image of his father grabbing a fistful of his own hair, pulling it up straight, and then taking a finger and tracing it over his forehead in a pantomime of a scalping had burned itself into Roy's young mind.

Chuck looked over to the old man. "Mattie? What happened to Mattie?"

"It wasn't good. Mattie came out of the cabin looking fer her husband. They grabbed her and hurt her bad, fellas. Did things to her even the Devil would be ashamed of, only that weren't the end of it.

"When they were done havin' their way with Mattie, they brought her back into the cabin and put her to bed. They didn't want Mattie to die. And not because they were upstandin' savages or nothin'. No. They wanted her to live because they wanted more of what they just got.

"And they got more when they came back durin' the full moon the next night.

"'Member when I told ya Mattie was a timid woman? Well, she'd gone through hell two nights in a row—her husband slaughtered and her gittin' beaten bad and used up. Somethin' snapped in her after that second night. Mattie changed. Musta' figured she was the only one who could get herself outta that jam. She planned on what she was gonna do, and then she waited fer 'em to return. She weren't disappointed. Like buffalo during ruttin' season, them Injun boys came back fer more."

"What'd she do?" Chuck asked, wide eyed and leaning toward Walter.

"She was sittin' upright in her bed, a blanket coverin' her lap when the three of 'em crashed through her front door. They didn't git more than halfway to her when she raised her shotgun and shot one of 'em in the crotch. The other two froze. That gave Mattie enough time to put a shell into the throat of the other one. The last Injun boy high-tailed it out of there 'fore she could get 'nother round into the chamber. He holed up behind the woodpile tryin' to figure out what to do. From there, he watched what Mattie did next.

"Mattie pulled that Indian she shot in the throat outta the cabin, and then laid him out by the barn. She went back and brought the other Injun out and laid him next to his dead brother. This one was still alive, moanin' and puttin' up a fight, though it didn't amount to nothin' considerin' how much of his middle was gone.

"She went back into the cabin one more time, came out with her shotgun, and then walked to the woodpile. She looked right into that Injun boy's eyes. She didn't raise her shotgun. Instead, she grabbed an ax lyin' by the woodpile, and then walked back to the two Injuns lyin' on the ground. Mattie lay the shotgun down and, with a fury that the Injun boy had never seen in any human being, she chopped his brothers inta pieces."

"Oh, my God," Roy said. Walter nodded and resumed his story.

"When finished, Mattie walked into the barn and came back with two long poles nestled in her arm. She used the ax to sharpen the ends and then pushed both poles inta the ground. After testin' 'em to make sure they were planted firmly, she went back to the bodies. She lifted the heads of those Injuns by their hair, and then she grabbed something else the Injun boy couldn't see and walked to the poles. Mattie then put everythin' but one head on the ground. With a grunt that musta echoed in that Injun boy's ears fer days, she pushed the head down onto one of them poles. She did the same with the other. When finished, she reached out and opened the mouths of both heads. She picked up the rest of what she brought over with her and then stuffed the mouths of those two dead Injuns with it."

Chuck and Roy stared at the old man. They didn't need him to explain what Mattie had used to gag those two heads.

"Mattie turned toward the Injun boy at the woodpile. She pointed at him and let loose a scream that musta traveled for miles. That Injun boy ran like the hounds of hell were after him. He said he ran all the way back to his daddy, Long Elk.

"Late the next day, Mattie had some visitors, some fellas from Spring Valley coming to check on her and her husband. A couple of passin' cowboys heard Mattie's scream the night before and reported it to the sheriff in town. They found Mattie actin' strange-like in her cabin, cleanin' up the blood and gittin the cabin in order like it was all in a day's work. They got her to tell her story, but they said it was like she was readin' it out of a book.

"The sheriff got a posse together and tracked down the remainin' Injun boy and Long Elk. They got someone who spoke Go-shute and, after gettin' the Injun boy drunk, they got all the details they needed to send him to trial. They hanged him.

"They let Long Elk go, though. The boy said his father knew nothin' 'bout the attacks on Mattie and her husband, and the sheriff couldn't prove that he did. But Long Elk swore revenge on Mattie for killin' his two boys and causin' the third to die at the end of a rope. Said he was gonna send one of the 'old ones' after her to make things right. Thing is, he never got his chance. As I heard it, Long Elk died a few days ago and we ain't never seen any 'old ones' 'round this way 'fore he passed."

"Walter," Chuck interrupted, "is Mattie still living on that spread? By herself?"

"Yup. I stopped by on my way here to fill up. She won't leave, not sure why, but she's never been the same since it happened. She stays away from people fer the most part, only heads into town when she got to. Word is that Brigham Young sends her money now and then and that's how she gets by, but no one really knows fer sure. Anyways, she'll give you water like I said, maybe even feed ya if yer hungry. But don't expect more. And when yer done, if you don't leave on yer own, she'll make sure ya do."

The three men fell silent, the weight of the old man's tale resting heavily on them. Eventually Roy spoke.

"It looks like we have little choice but to head to Mattie's spread. Hopefully, she'll show us the same kindness as she done you. We'll leave after we've had our fill, Walter. We don't want to cause her any more upset." Roy yawned and continued, "I wouldn't mind sitting and talking more with you some, but I'm baked and tired—I need sleep. I suspect you'll be up and leaving once dark falls, same as us. If you don't mind, we can finish any more talking we got then."

The old man nodded. The three of them spread out blankets and made themselves as comfortable as they could. Sleeping on the ground was nothing new for him, so Roy slept soundly.

When he woke, the sun had set, there was a chill in the air, and the moon was so full that he could see well enough to recall where he was and get his bearings. He sat up, stretched the sleep out of him, and groaned softly between yawns. He turned to his partner to wake him. Chuck was gone. So was the old man. Chuck's pack was on the ground but Walter's was missing. Roy glanced over to the Joshua tree and saw both their horses tied up, with Walter's saddle and pack on his horse. He hoped they were looking to catch a desert tortoise for dinner or, hell, maybe they just decided to relieve themselves at the same time. He put it out of his mind and rifled through his own pack for coffee grounds.

Roy gathered some loose brush and made a small fire. They

could spare the water since they were headed to Mattie's spread. After he poured water into the pot and placed it above the fire, he sat down and looked to where Chuck and the old man had been sleeping. He noticed a dark patch on the sand where Walter slept. He walked over and bent down. With one look, he had an idea what it was. When he ran his fingers over the stained sand, he could almost taste the copper on his lips. Blood—quite a bit of it—had soaked into the ground.

"Hey, partner."

Roy jumped when he heard the greeting.

Chuck approached him from the side of the rock formation, wiping his hands on a piece of cloth as he spoke. "It's okay," he said, "I took care of him. We got plenty of water now if Mattie's pump won't work."

Roy stared at him. "What did you do, Chuck?"

Grinning, Chuck reached down and removed a knife that hung from his side. "Used this." He looked down at the knife while turning it over in his hands. "It was quick—I don't expect he felt much."

Roy's throat constricted. "Why?"

"I told you why." With the moonlight shining down on them, Roy saw that Chuck's grin had vanished. Chuck cocked his head and asked, "You gotta problem with that, partner?"

"What did you do with the old man, Chuck?"

Chuck glared at Roy. "I buried him out in the sand, took his water bags and what food he had, and put them on my horse. I'm going to let his horse run, it won't last long in this heat. If anyone finds it, they'll think the old man took off on foot after his horse died and that he's lost in this desert. I'll ask you again, Roy—you got a problem with this?"

Roy had more than a few problems with it. He had given up everything he had to go out West with Chuck and strike it rich. Turns out his partner was a madman. And, he'd just made Roy an accessory to murder. Roy eyed the knife in Chuck's hand and came to a quick decision.

"No, I ain't got a problem with it."

Chuck's face relaxed and a smile formed on his lips. "Good. Let's get going. We've got a date with Mattie."

CHAPTER THREE

June 24, 1880

Roy and Chuck rode at an even pace toward Mattie's spread. Chuck led the way, having somehow gotten the directions from Walter before he killed him. Roy hoped that Walter had given Chuck phony directions, but it wouldn't have mattered much. One way or another, they would have found her spread.

Though Roy was worried about how this would play out, he wasn't too scared at this point. Chuck could have killed him at any time during their evening ride, but Roy had no idea how Chuck was going to handle the situation once they got to Mattie's.

When they had saddled up, Roy had checked his rifle and pistols and discovered that the bullets had been removed. When he asked Chuck about it, he was told that it was for insurance. There was little Roy could do or say. He would have to bide his time, convince Chuck that they were still partners, and then wait for an opportunity to get an upper hand. While he wasn't yet scared for himself, he couldn't say the same about Mattie.

He'll do something just as sick as what those Go-chutes did to her.

The two men spoke little as they rode. This gave Roy time to think about what might go down when they reached Mattie's spread. He played different scenarios in his head, but all of them ended in bloodshed.

With the rising sun cresting the horizon, the hue of the landscape brightened. Chuck brought his horse to a halt, and Roy had little choice but to do likewise. Chuck sat motionless on his saddle for a few moments, then raised a hand and pointed. Roy swung his head in that direction and saw a faint outline of a farmhouse—Mattie's spread.

"Here's what we're going to do, Roy," Chuck explained. "You're going to dismount, hand me the reins, and then you're going to walk the rest of the way to Mattie's. I'm going to ride ahead of you and check it out. I'll wait for you there."

Roy's eyes met Chuck's. Chuck grinned.

Roy remained calm. "The sun is up, it's going to get damned hot out here."

"Well, then, I suggest you hurry, Roy. I figure it'll take you about an hour to walk there. Drink some water now, and then you can grab some more at Mattie's pump."

Roy dismounted and handed Chuck the reins, which Chuck tethered to his own saddle. Roy lifted a water bag off his horse and drank as much as he could hold. As he was placing the water bag back onto the horse, he looked at Chuck, who was still grinning.

"Don't hurt her," Roy pleaded.

Chuck gazed down at him, his grin widening into a broad smile. "Hell, if everything goes right, Roy, it shouldn't hurt a bit. And don't you worry, partner—you'll get your turn."

Roy's stomach churned.

The sun beat down hard, and Roy could feel the heat rising from the sand. Adjusting his hat and loosening the top of his shirt, he began his trek toward Mattie's.

Despite the urge to cover the distance quickly, he walked. He knew he'd be a dead man in no time if he ran. He took slow, steady strides, hoping to God that he would outlast the sun's punishment. It didn't take long for sweat to ooze from his pores, sting his eyes, and flow into his ears. In minutes, his clothes were soaked. Sweat didn't bother Roy; he welcomed it. He knew if his body stopped sweating, he would be in trouble. He focused ahead, ignoring the discomfort as best he could.

Roy's pacing served him well. Though the sun's harsh rays drained his fluids, there was a good chance he could make it to Mattie's before passing out from dehydration. As he neared her spread, his gratitude about surviving gave way to despair. His thoughts turned to what Chuck would do to Mattie.

Roy had used his walking time to formulate a plan to subdue Chuck. Without a gun and weak from his walk, he had no illusions of success. His only hope was to get to his horse, remove a knife he had carried in his saddlebag, and then get the jump on Chuck.

A short distance away, Mattie's pump came into view. Roy plotted how he was going to get to the knife after he'd had his fill of water. He looked beyond the pump, trying to see where Chuck might have tied the horses.

The sound of a gunshot pierced his ears. It cracked through the dead air and echoed in every direction. He stopped, praying that it wasn't what he thought it was, but the noise repeated four more times. It took all of Roy's will not to collapse into the sand.

The gunshots sounded as if they had come from a pistol, not a shotgun. Although Mattie could have done the shooting, Roy was sure it was Chuck's handgun. He had little doubt that he would be the next target.

Gathering his remaining strength, Roy pushed himself to get to the pump as quickly as possible. The closer he got, the more he thought that at any moment one more shot would ring out, and he would never reach it.

The shot never came.

Contrary to what the old man had said, it only took a few tries before water flowed out of the pump. Roy dropped to his knees and pressed his face into the flowing water. He drank deeply.

Having his fill, Roy slumped onto the damp sand. Without warning, the hair on the back of Roy's neck stood up. *Could Chuck have snuck up on me?* He lifted his head. The feeling was uncanny, as if he were being watched. As he turned his head to look, something caught his eye. He hadn't noticed it on his run to the pump, but to his far right, a round, black object lay on the ground. Puzzled, he rose to his feet and moved toward the object.

A loud thud came from the cabin, diverting Roy's attention. He shook his head a few times, tossing away any notion of examining the object. He turned toward the cabin.

He saw nothing that would have caused the sound. To the right of the cabin he saw a lean-to with a hitching post. Tethered to the beam were both his and Chuck's horses. Roy's pulse quickened. He started toward the horses and saw something on the ground that caught his eye: an ax, covered in dust. He picked it up and examined it. The handle was short and stained yellow in places, but the head was solidly attached and the blade looked honed enough to do some damage.

Ax in hand, Roy crouched and ran to the horses. To his relief, no one had taken a shot at him.

Roy checked Chuck's saddlebags. The rifle was gone and there were no other guns. He then went through his own saddlebag, ignoring the rifle and Colts that hung from it knowing they were empty, and found the knife. It was small, but sharp. If he could get close enough to Chuck, pressing it against his throat would draw blood, and then, maybe, he could disarm him. For a brief moment the idea of taking both horses and leaving the spread entered his mind but he discarded the thought. If Mattie were still alive, he was her only chance for survival.

Hiding behind the horses, Roy took some time to decide how he would enter the cabin. The horses were skittish, leaving him exposed, so he did his best to calm them down. There was an odor in the air, akin to spoiled meat, and Roy thought it was upsetting them. When he looked around to trace its source, his eyes rested on a small corral. Flies buzzed in panicked swarms around the remains of a horse. It rested on the sand in large pieces and was left to rot. From the smell, he thought that it had been dead for a while. If so, wild animals and birds should have devoured the carcass by now. Yet, it was still there. There was no time for him to dwell on it.

Roy ran to the back corner of the cabin hoping to see a window, or even better, a door. He was in luck on both counts. Pressing himself flat against the wall, he proceeded to the window and craned his neck to look inside.

It might have been a small bedroom, but it was hard to tell in the sun's glare. Shielding his eyes, he blinked away the sunspots and then focused. The furniture was upended, shards of broken glass littered the floor, and women's clothing was strewn about. Roy sighed with relief—there was no blood. He eased his way to the door, placed his ear to it, and heard nothing. He removed a thick oak plank that had been wedged between the doorknob and the ground, tossing it aside. *Was Chuck trying to keep Mattie trapped inside?* The door opened easily. Roy leaned forward and peered in.

He spied a hallway littered with discarded housewares and broken furniture with a path cleared through its center. There was no door at the other end which led into a room. Roy entered and propped the door open with the oak plank for additional light and for a fast retreat if needed. He saw a lock on the inside of the door and was thankful it had not been latched.

He walked into in the hallway, holding the knife tightly in one hand and the ax in the other. A few steps in, he heard low, muffled sounds coming from the room. It was a familiar sound—it reminded him of pigs when eating slop.

Lost in concentration, he bumped into some debris along the path. He froze as the sounds stopped. He heard what could have been a door closing, but he couldn't be sure. After waiting an eternity, he stepped lightly up the path. Reaching the end, he inched forward to see around the corner. Roy was unable to move. It took all of his willpower not to vomit.

Roy looked into the room and met Chuck's eyes. They were resting on the floor, atop a scatter rug. The rest of his head was lying upside down a few feet behind them. What remained of his neck was mangled and bloodied, the flesh looking as though it had been stretched to the point of tearing. Roy's first thought was that Chuck's head had been pulled off his body, but after looking around the room, he came to a different conclusion.

Chuck's remains, mostly arms and legs, littered the floor. The limbs varied in size, but all had one thing in common—large chunks of flesh were missing, exposing bone. The wounds were ragged and fresh, blood pooled beneath them.

Chuck's head wasn't torn off...it was chewed off.

Mattie or no Mattie, Roy wanted no part of this. He backed slowly into the hallway, keeping the knife and ax at the ready when the door behind him shut.

He turned and rushed the door, slamming his shoulder into it, but it refused to open. Shaken from the impact, he had dropped both his weapons. He rubbed the pain out of his shoulders and tried kicking the door, but it held fast. It was blocked solidly from the outside—someone must have wedged the oak plank back into place.

Roy bent down to collect the knife and ax, and then faced the living area. He made his way back through the hallway, and at the end, he paused to survey the room. There were two windows along the far wall and between them stood a door—his means of escape from this slaughterhouse.

He crept through the room, careful to avoid body parts as he made his way. As he approached the door, he saw Chuck's torso, or what was left of it, leaning against a rocking chair. Several broken ribs with ribbons of meat dangled from the spine, many of which had been gnawed on. Those pig-like, slop-eating noises he had heard earlier came back to him.

What in hell could have mutilated Chuck that fast?

There were streams of a yellow liquid covering the floor and streaking the walls, some of which had collected into small puddles. It reminded him of blood. *What the hell bleeds yellow?*

He recalled the five gunshots he heard while making his way to the pump. The thought chilled him, and he picked up his pace.

As he reached for the door, he held out the knife and pushed the point against it. The door moved forward without resistance, but only a few inches. With a quick look behind him, he pushed the door all the way open, and then bolted through it. After he cleared the threshold, he ran headfirst into someone.

Or something.

It was soft and spongy but firm enough to stand its ground. Roy bounced off it, lost his balance, and landed on his ass, his legs askew. He lifted his arms to ward off a possible attack, slashing at anything coming for him, but the knife and ax sliced empty air. It took a few seconds for him to rein in his fear and confusion, take a deep breath, and then look up. For the first time since he was a child, Roy screamed.

It stared down at him.

Tall and muscular with dark green skin, it stood before him wearing a dress so torn and tattered that it might as well have been naked. What remained of the garment clung around its waist, soaked in red. The monster's breasts were large and hung heavily, but they lacked nipples. In their place were small, ivory-colored discs. In the center of its right breast were two small puncture holes oozing yellow liquid. Below the breast, three similar holes leaked.

The monster stood on two long green tubes that bore no resemblance to human legs. Another green tube hung from its right shoulder alongside its torso. Ivory-colored discs, like those on the breasts, were aligned in neat rows along its length. On its left side, a nub of flesh, only inches long, extended from the shoulder. Where fingers and toes should have been, five tentacles darted in the air like snakes hunting flies. Each tentacle was over a foot long, their bodies as thin as pencils and as flexible as rope. At their tips were triangles, black in color and three or four times wider than their bodies. The triangles opened and closed rapidly, and Roy glimpsed smaller triangles embedded within them. They were bone white with an occasional flash of red. The cold realization settled into his mind when he saw that they were bloodstained—Chuck.

Roy needed to get off his ass, run back into the house, and slam the door on this abomination. That might give him some time to think his way out of this mess. Would the monster pounce if he made a move? Would it be his eyes lying on the scatter rug? Roy lifted his gaze and peered into the monster's face.

Its head was oval shaped, smooth, and as hairless as the rest of its body. Five tentacles, identical to the ones attached to each of its limbs, hovered over its crown, their triangles pointing in Roy's direction. Unlike the others, they were motionless.

Are they studying me?

The skin covering the monster's face was wrinkled, as if worn from age or exposure to the sun. Its mouth was small, half the size of a human's, but its lips were full and shapely. Though he had no way of knowing, the holes on both sides of the monster's head must have functioned as ears. Above the lips was a small bump, perfectly round with a tiny hole in its center. If it was a nose, Roy marveled that it could breathe through such a small opening.

The monster's eyes were the most human trait it possessed. They were almond shaped, with black pupils floating in a sea of white. Roy stared into them, desperately searching for a hint of humanity.

The monster's eyes shifted and locked on Roy.

Roy couldn't look away. A chill rippled through his spine and his hands trembled. When the monster blinked, Roy flinched and cried out. It leaned forward without breaking eye contact, then blinked again. A moment passed, and then the monster lowered its eyelids and stood still.

It was Roy's turn to blink.

Is this a test?

Roy swallowed hard, took a few deep breaths, and then he waited. His wait wasn't long.

The monster's eyelids snapped open. Roy's heart pounded so hard his chest burned as if it was on fire. The urge to run was overwhelming, but he stayed—he had no idea what this thing was capable of. He studied the monster and saw that its eyes had changed. They were less intense. *Softer, maybe?* Roy had no idea if he was overthinking this or not, but did he see anguish in its eyes? Could it be the hint of humanity he was looking for? Cocking his head, he asked a single, one-word question.

"Mattie?"

Roy wasn't prepared for the answer.

The monster's upper limb sprang toward him so fast that he barely registered its movement. It wrapped around his throat, the tube as flexible as he had imagined it to be. Tentacles darted through the air, snapping their teeth rapidly, loudly, beating a high-pitched rhythm in his ears. The tube constricted, and then pulled, lifting Roy off the porch. His feet flailed as he struggled to breathe. When his head was level with that of the monster, it pulled him closer until their faces almost touched. Their eyes locked, and when Roy's went wide with fear, the tube squeezed harder. His chest heaved with the effort to breathe.

He was too close to use the ax effectively, but not the knife. He gripped the hilt tighter, swung his arm up, and plunged the blade deep into the monster's breast. Although the knife sank to its hilt, the pressure on Roy's throat remained steady. Roy grit his teeth, tensed his shoulders, and then pushed down on the knife, slicing green skin as far as his reach would allow. When he could cut no farther, he twisted the knife, and then pulled up. He sawed at the monster's flesh until he felt a give in its hold. But it was not enough to allow the air back into his lungs.

The strength in Roy's arm waned and he was on the verge of passing out. He pulled the knife from the wound, lifted it over his head, and plunged it deep into the monster's forehead. The grip around his throat held tight.

Exhausted and out of breath, Roy's mind turned cloudy. As his thoughts faded, his eyes closed and his body went limp. His grip on the knife relaxed and his arm fell to his side. He floated into darkness and welcomed the peace that death promised.

The impact of his body slamming to the porch floor brought him back to consciousness.

On his back, confused and gasping for breath, Roy's sense of self-preservation kicked in. His elbows and heels dug into the floorboards, propelling him backward as he crawled away. His head slammed against the cabin's wall, bringing him to a stop. He pushed himself up into a sitting position and leaned back, tightening his grasp on the ax. Gasping for air, he reached with a hand to massage his throat.

When Roy's breathing calmed, he pulled himself together and concentrated on the monster. It hadn't moved. Worse, it appeared to have suffered no ill effects from the knife wounds. Roy sighed and hung his head. When he looked up, the monster was in motion.

The arm tube moved to the knife lodged in its forehead. The tentacles maneuvered around the knife, their triangles bobbing up and down, their teeth chattering. With one mind, they inspected the injury. Satisfied, they made their move.

The triangles plunged into the wound, surrounding the knife and burrowing deep. They re-emerged, dripping yellow, and then hovered around the injury with their teeth clamped around the blade. In unison, the triangles opened, and the knife dropped to the ground.

Roy shook his head. *How in hell am I going to defeat this thing?* He stared hard at it, scanning its body, looking for weaknesses.

Ungainly as it appeared, Roy knew he couldn't run from it. Earlier, the monster had been able to bar the rear hallway door and get to the front of the house in no time. Roy would lose the race if he took off running. He concentrated on the monster's leg tubes. He didn't understand how they were capable of motion as they looked too flexible to support its weight. He couldn't imagine how it even managed to stand. An idea began to take form, but before he could think it through, the monster gave him a demonstration of how mobile it actually was.

Its leg tubes began to undulate. The texture of the skin went from smooth to rough, its spongy flesh turning solid and bulky. The tubes hardened, as if air was pumped into them and they bent outward at their midpoint.

Knees! It can make its own knees!

The tentacles at the end of its leg tubes were in motion, wrapping themselves around its legs and then biting to secure their hold.

They don't want to be crushed when this thing starts walking!

The whole transformation took seconds.

The monster lifted one of its leg tubes and stepped toward Roy. The movement was not hurried. It was in no rush to reach him.

Roy estimated the distance between them around six feet. It would take only three more steps before it reached him. The monster advanced, and Roy acted.

Roy screamed at the top of his lungs. It was a battle cry, so loud and so unexpected, that it caused the monster to pause in mid-step. Roy raised the ax, maneuvering it behind him until it hit the wall. Crying out once more, he swung it forward with everything he had.

The ax found its target.

The blade severed the tentacles coiled around the left leg tube. They fell to the floor, scattering blindly like bugs exposed from under a rock, shuddering as they died. But Roy's swing wasn't hard enough and the ax jammed halfway in. He went to his knees and worked feverishly to pull it out, his muscles aching and his face dripping in sweat from the effort. After several tugs, it came free. Roy pulled his arm back, ready for another swing when from the corner of his eye he caught a motion above him. It was the arm tube. Like arrows in flight, the tentacles darted toward him in formation, their triangles snapping, their teeth dripping yellow.

Adrenalin surged through Roy, and without much thought, he swung the ax, cutting through the air like lightning over a desert plain. The ax connected high, close to the monster's shoulder, slicing through the flesh. The arm tube was severed clean.

Caught off guard by the ease of his swing, Roy lost his balance, catching a blur of green as he fell. The severed tube dropped to the floorboards as Roy toppled over onto his belly, his face inches from the severed limb. He was certain that it was in its death throes as it convulsed. But there was no time to savor the victory. Confident, and with ax still in hand, Roy stood.

The monster hadn't moved other than planting both leg tubes on the porch floor. The tentacles on top of its head were stretched fully and hovered over the injured shoulder. They were silent, their incessant chattering gone. It took Roy a moment to understand that the monster must have been confused. It shifted its weight back and forth between its two leg tubes, testing them maybe to see how much strength the wounded leg tube had.

Roy didn't wait for the monster to figure it out.

He crouched and prepared to strike again. He raised the ax, and then swung it so hard that if he had missed his target, the momentum would have sent him sailing across the porch.

But he didn't miss, and this time the ax sliced all the way through. Roy sidestepped and swung at the other leg tube. The ax sailed through it and out the other side easily.

The results were immediate.

The monster's torso teetered for a moment and then toppled backward, falling from the porch, landing on its back. A small cloud of grainy sand floated in the air upon impact. The severed leg tubes remained standing, their weight anchoring them to the floorboards. Yellow fluid jetted from their stumps, soaking Roy and everything around him. He reached out his arm and used the ax to head butt one, and then the other stump. They fell over spasming. Once they stilled, Roy walked off the porch and watched the blood run out of them. Then a movement caught his eye.

The tentacles attached to the monster's head were still alive. They were slower, and their triangles snapped without conviction. They would die shortly so he turned his attention to the monster's face.

Mattie's face.

Her lips moved. She tried to speak, but Roy couldn't hear the words. He debated bending over and putting an ear closer to her when pain exploded in his right leg. One of the tentacles had managed to find enough strength to attach itself to his calf. Furious, he brought the ax down and severed it from the back of Mattie's head. The triangle released its clamp, dropping to the sand. Cursing, Roy stomped on it, first with one leg, then jumping up and down on it with both feet. When he was through, he sneered at the carcass and kicked it away.

Roy picked up his pant leg to gauge the damage. While he examined the bite, a raspy sound behind him made him jump. Turning, he saw that it was coming from Mattie. He smoothed his pant leg down and approached until he stood directly above her. He bent low and listened, but he still couldn't make out her words. He focused on her lips and tried to match their movement with the sounds. Finally, he understood what she was trying to tell him.

"Kill me, kill me, kill me..."

Roy straightened up and looked deeply into Mattie's eyes. Finally, he replied. "No fucking problem."

Roy lifted the ax and brought it down hard between her eyes. Her head split in two, the halves separated until her ear holes were flat against the ground. In a volcanic rage, Roy continued to chop at Mattie's body and didn't stop until he was exhausted. All that remained of Mattie were small, green pieces of spongy flesh, some dotted with slivers of ivory, all of it soaked in a yellow broth.

Roy dropped the ax and stood before the carnage. Sweat dripped from his forehead, and for the first time since he had drunk from Mattie's pump, he noticed the heat. He was hurt, he was tired, and he was covered from head to toe in yellow. He turned to the pump, taking a moment to stare at it. It hadn't been that long since he had drunk from it. He staggered to it, his shoulders slumped and his head hanging.

He jacked the handle a few times. It gave up its wealth and he kneeled under the spigot and let the water pour over him. He let the water wash the blood and sand away before he opened his mouth. When he had drunk his fill, he slumped to the ground, his back resting against the pump. He itched where the triangle had bitten him but he was too tired to examine his leg. He needed rest, to gather his strength before he left the spread, and to find some shade. He'd look at his leg later.

Try as he might, he couldn't relax. His body remained tense and his neck was stiff. Something was making him feel uneasy and he thought he saw the reason—the black object on the ground that he had seen earlier.

What the hell is that, and why am I so troubled by it?

Roy should have been terrified at what he saw next, but he was too tired. A weary curiosity was the best he could manage.

Two hands, human hands, had thrust up from the object with all ten fingers stretched skyward. They flexed a few times as if chasing away a long-suffering stiffness. The fingers wrapped themselves around the lip of the object and a head rose from behind. Its hair was grey. A face rose into view—it was old, wrinkled, and framed by a pair of braids. It belonged to an Indian.

The Indian rose high until its arms were visible. He leaned forward, lifting a leg out of the object and setting it on the ground. Balancing himself, he climbed out. When the Indian was free of the hole, he stood naked on the sand, his back and his knees bent forward. The Indian took a moment to survey his surroundings, then, as if sniffing prey, he turned to face Mattie's cabin. He walked toward it, grimacing in pain. When he reached the spot where Mattie lay, the Indian stopped and studied the ground, and he peered at the scattered pieces of her body. When the Indian had seen enough, he straightened up as best he could, and then turned to face Roy.

Roy should have reacted in some way to the Indian's gaze, but after what he had been through, he was too tired to do anything.

The old Indian walked toward him and instead of confronting him, the Indian walked past him to the hole. When he reached it, he turned to gaze at the exhausted cowboy once more. The Indian looked as if he were about to say something, but if he were going to, he never had the chance to get the words out.

Two green tubes erupted from the hole, one of them wrapping itself around the Indian's neck, the other around his waist. With a yank as quick as the blink of an eye, they dragged him back into the hole.

Roy watched stone-faced as the hole grew smaller until it vanished. He shook his head and thought of the tale Walter had told them.

Long Elk.

Roy stood. His clothes were dry and they felt a bit stiff. He looked in the direction that he and Chuck had ridden from, and searched for an outcropping of rocks. He saw one in the far distance.

Roy was going to get his horse, fill the water bags, and get the hell out of there. After he'd had some sleep in the shade of the outcropping, he was going to head back to Kansas. Gold or no gold, if California was anything like this, he wanted no part of it.

I always have wanted to write a noir tale—a dark, atmospheric story with the three B's of the genre: booze, bullets and babes. I struggled to find a suitable plot, but one morning it came to me.

A concrete bridge spans a river running through our town. Headed to work one day, I saw an old man fishing off the bridge. There was nothing special about him, but the scene stayed with me. My commute is 90 minutes each morning, and by the time I pulled into the parking lot, I had the basics of a story line in my head. It was published in Anthology-Year One, and I am grateful for editor Mark Wholley's input on the type of weapons used in the story as well as the nickname for one of the characters. Mark also told me it was his dad's favorite story in the anthology.

THE OLD MAN

I called him "the old man" though he wasn't much older than me. Maybe it's my ego talking here, but from a respectable distance we didn't look like two guys who had just reached retirement age. Hell, if you cocked your head to one side and squinted you might even say we looked alike, though his ears stuck out farther than mine and his hair was a bit grayer. And, yeah, maybe our marathon running days were behind us, but we were still both in pretty good shape physically, and I bet he could have handled himself quite nicely in a tough situation, if it came down to that.

We'd met in Goffstown, on the first day of fishing season in New Hampshire, when he saw me casting a line from the concrete bridge spanning the Piscataquog River. He wandered across it and over my way with a bamboo pole draped over his shoulder, a tackle box dangling from one hand and a smile that could put a crying baby at ease. We made small talk about trout, bass, and catfish. After a while the discussion turned to ourselves. We were both recently retired and had some time on our hands. And, in a town as small as Goffstown, in the warmer months anyway, that time was spent with those hands wrapped around a fishing pole.

We continued to run into each other often after that first meeting. Before you knew it, it'd become a routine where we'd meet up every morning at the bridge, drop our lines into the water, and spend the morning feeding the fish and passing the time together. When we would grow tired of re-hooking bait, or if the fish stopped biting, we would head over to the Lion's Club's popcorn stand in the center of town and grab a bag of that greasy stuff along with a drink to wash it down. Then we'd mosey on back to the bridge and sit on the benches that overlooked the water. We'd shoot the breeze about the news, the local gossip, and of course, the weather.

He'd talk about anything, well, anything except his past. We spent most of our summer days on that bridge throwing fish back into the river and kibitzing, though I did learn that he was once married, had no kids, and had lived in Goffstown for only a short time. He used to rib me about my ten-minute drive every morning and often reminded me about the empty apartment next to his. He lived by himself in a small apartment off Church Street, only a few blocks away from the bridge. Without fail, he would nod his head in agreement and smile when I replied that I had a rental house that was tucked into the woods and that I had liked my privacy. No way was I going to trade that away just for a shorter commute to a fishing spot. Of course, he meant well. He was just a lonely old guy looking for someone to chum around with.

So, one morning we're both sitting there on one of the benches overlooking the river, stuffing our faces with popcorn and discussing the finer points of Raquel Welch, when I heard a muffled sound from behind us. Though it initially triggered some warning bells, I ignored it, thinking it had come from one of the cars passing by on the bridge. I looked down at the bag tucked between my legs, intending to grab another handful of popcorn, when I pulled up short. I noticed something odd—it was streaked with splashes of red.

Confused, I turned to face the old man. I saw his arm; it was hanging in midair between his knees and mouth, frozen, with a fistful of popcorn clutched tightly in his hand. It, too, was soaked in red, as was the rest of his hand.

Alarmed, I looked closer, and saw that his eyes were wide open and staring straight ahead. At his throat was a hole, as big as a quarter, blood squirting out of it like a ruptured hose. Then, slowly, the old man turned to look at me. The corners of his mouth were sunk and his brow was wrinkled. He tried to speak, but all that came out was a gagging noise. Then his eyes closed and he tilted, sliding toward me. As he leaned against my shoulder, his blood dripped onto my thigh and soaked into the bag of popcorn.

I pushed the old man upright and turned to look behind us. A young guy in an overcoat stood there, a look of satisfaction on his face as he stared at the back of the old man's head. He was holding a handgun. I recognized it as a Walther, the tip of its suppressor still smoking.

The young guy turned and faced me. When our eyes met, he gasped and took a step backward. Then he swung the gun toward me and squeezed the trigger.

Nothing happened, so he tried it again. Still, the gun didn't fire.

He stood for a moment, stunned. With panic in his eyes, he quickly lowered the gun and ran toward the road, crossing over the bridge. Twice he looked back at me. Each time, I swear, I saw anguish on his face.

Though it pained me to do so, I left the old man there on the bench. Before leaving I had gone through his pockets and removed his wallet, throwing it into my tackle box. Then, I gathered up my gear and headed straight to my car. I had to get home, and get there fast. I knew that the old man's murder might be the biggest crime this town had ever seen, so I wasn't surprised as I drove by the police station on the way to my rental house and noticed a flurry of activity. Cruisers were pulling out of the parking lot with their sirens wailing and their blue lights flashing.

With the amount of foot traffic around the bridge I had figured it wouldn't be all that long before the old man was found. I had hoped for at least a few minutes' delay before the cops responded, then a few hours more before they discovered who he was, and who might have been his fishing buddy. The clock had started ticking, and I needed to get back home.

There was precious little in the house that I needed, but I did have a stash there with traveling money and a gun. I was in desperate need of both.

When I pulled into the driveway I noticed right away that someone had been in the house. Whenever I leave, I put a small garden gnome at the outer edge of the back door, and I do the same thing with a small flower pot by the front door. Anyone entering would displace these items by a few inches when opening the doors. I saw that the garden gnome had been pushed to the side. I turned the car off and headed up the back stairs.

After crossing a small deck to reach the door, I stood off to one side, jiggled my keys a bit, and then, reaching out, slipped the house key into the lock. Sure enough, splinters of wood exploded from the door and two holes appeared in its center where I should have been standing.

I dropped down to the deck grunting, making as much noise as possible. Then I got back up and stood to the side of the door again, this time flattening myself against the wall. I got lucky; I didn't have to wait long for him to make his move.

The door opened slowly. I saw the tip of the suppressor inch its way through the opening and, as I expected, it was angled down. Seconds later the Walther came into view. Then the hand that held it. I noticed it was shaking.

I quickly grabbed the guy's exposed wrist and slammed it against the doorframe. I expected to hear another muffled shot, but the force of the blow caused him to release the gun and it clattered onto the deck. I jumped away from the wall and gave him a quick knee to the groin. He doubled over and I followed it up with a right to his jaw. Moaning, he dropped like a lead sinker. This was too easy.

I kicked the gun from the deck into the house, then grabbed the guy by the collar and dragged him into the living room. After depositing him on the floor, I went to the bookshelf, opened a hollowed-out, leather-bound copy of the King James Bible, and removed the cash and a snub-nosed pistol. Pointing the gun at the intruder, I told him to get his ass off of the floor and sit in the easy chair. Groaning, he rose and plopped down onto the cushions. I took a few seconds to look him over. As I suspected, he was just a kid, mid-twenties at best.

"So, Sammy's sending babies now to do his dirty work." I said to him. Then, sounding somewhat offended, I added, "Freaking amateurs."

"I'm no amateur," he replied, reacting to the disgust in my voice.

"The hell you ain't. Those misfires back at the bridge? I'm betting it's because you used reloads. They are prone to misfiring with a dirty chamber." I looked back at the two holes in the door, "You must have figured that out." Then I added with a chuckle, "A bit too late, though."

The kid sighed and hung his head.

"And you screwed up royally by mistaking my fishing buddy for me."

With his head still down he whispered, "Yeah, I thought it would be easier doing you at the bridge than here."

"So, after you messed up the hit, you came here anyway and waited for me. I saw the look on your face when you ran. You knew that Sammy was going to have your balls if he found out you killed the wrong guy."

I barely heard the word "yeah" when he muttered it again.

Now it was my turn to sigh.

Slowly the kid lifted his head and looked me in the eyes. "What did you do to Sammy to piss him off so much?" His hands were shaking again.

I debated whether or not to tell him. The kid got himself involved with a lot more than he could handle and now he was going to pay the price. The least I could do was answer his question.

"I worked muscle for him, collecting on bad debts. Easy stuff, mostly numbers. I usually didn't have to hurt anyone, too badly anyway. Maybe a broken bone here or there, but they usually paid up after that. Then one day Sammy sent me out to a house with a new guy to collect from some loser who owed Sammy a grand. I didn't know this new guy, called himself Shark, but if Sammy wanted him to come along I figured, what the hell. We go to the loser's house and guess what? He ain't got the money. Well, Shark went ape. He started throwing furniture around the living room, busted the TV and then he started beating on the poor guy. Then we heard a voice.

"It was someone in the back of the house calling, 'Daddy.' So Shark went to check. He comes back dragging a little girl by her hair and he tells the loser that he's gonna kill her if he doesn't pay up.

"Well, this wasn't part of the game and I didn't like it. I told Shark to lay off. He ignored me and put the gun to the girl's head. I don't know, maybe he just meant it as a bluff, but something went wrong. The girl started wiggling in his arms and then the gun went off. He blew her brains out all over the living room.

"Shark let go of her body and she crumpled to the floor. He just stood there, with no expression, looking down at her. There was blood and bits of brain covering his face. Then, with that same, damn, blank expression, he looked up at the loser, and then he shot him in the head too.

"Shark turned to me, grinned, and said, 'Can't have any witnesses.'

"I'd seen a lot of crap in my time, kid. Done a lot of crap, too. But I never killed a kid or offed someone over short money. I walked up to Shark, took the gun from his hand, and stared at him for a second. Then, I put a bullet right between his eyes."

The kid in the chair looked at me, his face caught somewhere between a grimace and confusion. Then he said, "So? What's the big deal? Sammy should have been happy you took care of the situation."

"Normally he would have," I replied. "It turned out Shark was Sammy's nephew. To tell you the truth, even if I'd known, I would have done him anyway. I had worked for Sammy for quite a while and he liked me, so he gave me a head start. He told me, 'Family is family,' and that he couldn't let anyone get away with killing family."

We were both quiet for a few seconds, the kid staring me down and me trying to wipe the memories from my head. Finally he asked me, "What now?"

"It's time for me to move on. I had a few good years here anyway. But you, hell, you're screwed, kid."

I leaned forward, aimed the snub-nosed at him, and fired. Then, I fired three more times.

I put one bullet in each of his knees and elbows. There was no way he was walking or crawling out of the house. I kicked the Walther into the kitchen, just in case he somehow managed to worm his way across the floor after I left. His prints would be on it, so the police would have no trouble tying him to the murder of the old man and, with any luck, the kid would have spilled his guts and that would have taken care of Sammy, too.

I figured the shots would have the cops here soon, so I hurried to the car and drove off, heading south. I was going to miss that old man. He was a good fishing partner and I'm sure we would have stayed friends even after fishing season ended. In a way he saved my life, and for that I'm grateful.

It's funny how things work out. Here I am talking to you with a pole in my hand, fishing on another bridge in some small town that's over 300 miles away from Goffstown. And I'm in the same damn situation as I was in back in Goffstown.

When I took the old man's wallet, I had planned on tossing it out somewhere on my way down here. But after thinking about it, I decided to use his identification. I could become him for a while. At least until the heat blew over. We looked enough alike, and he didn't have any family to worry about, so it seemed like the thing to do. Anyway, I guess I should've dug a little deeper into the old man's past. Who would have believed two different mob guys on the run would pick the same small town in New Hampshire to hide in?

I can see you're no kid. You're no freaking amateur either. And that Glock you're pointing at me? I'd bet you're using match-grade ammo and not reloads. And, I bet that chamber is as clean as a whistle. No way that gun misfires. You've got more damn smarts than that kid Sammy sent, that's for sure. Look, I know you don't believe my story, but it's the truth. I'm not the guy you're looking for. He's that old man on the bench that Sammy's kid capped back in New Hampshire a month ago.

I can see by your eyes you don't believe me. Hell then, will you do an old man a favor? I'm going to turn around and face the water. All I want to do is to throw one more line and go out doing what I love. Will you do that for me?

Thanks, young fella.

This story came about from a prompt by Keith Minnion for a writing exercise at the Horror World website. What I remember the most about this story is something that occurred when I presented it to my writers group. When it was my turn for the critique, they had all looked at me in silence. Finally, one of them said, "You have found your voice." This story was published in Epitaphs, a New England Horror Writers anthology, edited by Tracey Carbone.

THE BURIAL BOARD

With a start, Turner rapidly raised his chin. Had his ears caught the tail end of a groan?

Struggling to keep his eyes open, Turner swung his head in a wide arc surveying the loft in an attempt to locate the origin of the sound. As the fog in his mind receded he cursed silently, taking himself to task for falling asleep. *Did I dream it*, he wondered? The sound was slight, distant. The barn could be settling, he reasoned, or maybe it was a sudden wind gust.

Turner shook his upper body, hoping to chase away the fatigue and the bite of the cold. He sat motionless in his chair and listened. After a moment he was confident the sound was of no consequence and his eyes settled on his wife's body and the burial board to which she had been bound. As he gazed upon her, his mind wandered.

Though Mary rested on it now, it was not the first time the burial board had been employed. He had come by the board just one week shy of Christmas in 1818. They had not celebrated the holidays that year, nor since. Turner had acquired the board when the milk sickness claimed Nancy, his eight-year-old daughter.

He recalled his wife's concern when Nancy began to appear weak and listless. Then the poor girl stopped voiding, resulting in painful stomach aches and the loss of her appetite. Soon after, her breath was so bad it was a struggle just to get close enough to tend to her. At that point Turner went to town and fetched the doctor. The news was devastating.

The doctor told them that she had The Slows, a disease that came with drinking milk from tainted cows feeding on white snakeroot. The doctor wondered why Nancy was the only one affected by the disease and Turner explained that he and Mary did not drink cow's milk; they preferred goat's milk, but since their daughter enjoyed cow's milk they would sometimes trade off with the neighbors. The doctor had prescribed Castoris to help Nancy regain some strength, and sarsaparilla for her constipation and stomach problems, but he could prescribe no cure. Days later they had learned that their neighbors had succumbed to the disease. It was no more than a week after the doctor's visit when Nancy had passed. Mary took her death hard, as did Turner.

Winter that year had come not only early, but cruelly. The snow was already knee-high, and the air so cold that the lakes and ponds had long frozen over. They would have to wait until spring to bury their daughter. The decision was made to place her in the barn, up in the loft, until the first thaw when they could give her a proper burial. Mary had insisted that Nancy be placed on a Christian burial board. Though he argued against it as their money was tight, he finally let her have her head.

Early in the morning, only three days after Nancy's passing, Turner removed the contents from their coin jar and placed it in his purse. He had no idea how much a burial board would cost, but he suspected that the meager contents of the jar wouldn't be enough to purchase a proper one. Unsure of what was to come, he saddled his mount and began the long and arduous journey into town. It had taken half a day when he had brought the doctor to his home, so he allowed himself that much time plus a little extra to find a board. Through no fault of his own, he soon discovered that he had miscalculated badly. The storm hit when he was halfway to town.

Between the high winds and blinding snow, Turner knew trouble had found him. He had lost his bearings in the whiteout and his horse protested its every step. He thought about turning back, but he had no idea in which direction to turn. He dismounted and grabbed the horse's reins; he needed to find shelter soon.

Though he'd thought about it often over the last two years, he still had no idea how he had found his way to the shack.

It had appeared out of nowhere. The simple fact was that he had walked right into it, striking his head against one of its sidewalls. Using his hands to follow the wall, he turned two corners until he came to a door. Turner pushed at it and was surprised at how easily it opened. He led his horse through the doorway and, once inside, he slammed it shut. He fell to the floor with his back sliding against the door and stayed there until he could catch his breath. After a few moments, he realized there was enough dim light coming from two windows on the opposite wall to study his surroundings.

Spying a lantern hanging from a peg, he lifted himself up off the floor and removed it. He found a box of matches on a shelf beside it so he removed his gloves and set the lantern to burning. What he saw in the shack confused him. Not only was it larger than he imagined, but it looked to be a gathering place of sorts.

Near the center of the room, there were a series of chairs placed in an odd, circular configuration, around what Turner took to be a crude altar. The altar was a simple affair consisting of a long, thick, ebony plank set on a pair of stone pillars. Turner placed the lantern directly above the altar and realized a small cross had been carved through the center of the plank. Though Turner was not a religious man, he was however, a practical one. He came to the conclusion quickly that he had found the burial board for his daughter.

Outdoors, the storm raged for a few hours longer, and then, as abruptly as it had begun, it quit. Turner prepared for his trip back home. After leading his horse out of the shack, he removed the plank from the pillars and secured one end of a rope around its length. He left the contents of his purse on one of the pillars and then carried the plank outdoors. Turner tied the other end of the rope to his horse's saddle. Unsure of his location, he took a chance on which direction to travel. His choice served him well. He quickly found some landmarks and made it home, the board dragging behind him, just as the sun was setting. That night, he and Mary placed their daughter in the loft and strapped her to the board.

Later that evening, Mary had the worst nightmares that Turner could ever recall her having. When she woke, all she could remember of her dreams was a groaning. She told him that it sounded like dry wood straining before it broke. Still in a daze and not quite awake, she had insisted on checking the barn and then dashed out of the house. Soon after, Turner heard her screams.

He rushed to the loft where he found Mary weeping over the burial board. Pushing her aside, he saw the board was empty, their daughter's body missing. The two straps he had used to tie her down were still secured to the board and not damaged. The loft appeared to be undisturbed and there were no signs of torn clothing or body parts. Checking the outside of the barn, the only tracks in the snow he noticed was theirs. It was as if her body had simply vanished. His wife was never the same after that night. With her mental health declining over the past two years, Turner was not shocked—in fact, he felt relief—when he awoke this morning, the second anniversary of their daughter's death, to find Mary hanging from a beam in front of the fireplace.

Now here he sat in the loft, conducting a vigil over his wife's body, repeatedly recalling the circumstances that had brought him here. Finally, he wept. When his tears were exhausted and he thought sleep was warranted, he heard it. The groaning. It was subtle and intermittent, but it was there. It reminded Turner of the sound of a lake in late March when its surface was cracking, just before ice-out, when the thaw began; he knew something powerful was happening out there, warning him away, even if he couldn't see it.

The volume and frequency of the groaning increased. When he realized the sound was coming from the burial board, his spine stiffened. Staring at the board, his eyes grew wide. The board had begun to move.

While the center of the board was firmly planted on the floor, its ends were vibrating, as though straining to lift themselves. The volume of the groaning increased, to the point where it was almost deafening, and the pain in his ears became so severe that Turner thought they might be bleeding. Mary's body began to jerk wildly, mimicking the motions of the board. Her head and feet were struggling to rise, but the straps that had secured her to the plank held tightly. Turner could only stare in disbelief when, after a series of violent tugs, the middle section of her body began a jerky descent into the board. The two ends of her body strained against the straps. Finally, they forcibly slipped through the restraints and were pulled toward one another, forcing her upper body and legs into a V as they followed the rest of her down into the board. The sounds of bones splintering joined the cacophony of groaning when her knees were violently thrust against her skull. The impact caused her head to turn toward him and her eyes were forced open. Though they were milky and devoid of life, he felt certain they followed him as the remainder of her body was pulled down into the board.

Turner's paralysis broke. He rushed from the chair and stood above the burial board. He saw no trace of his wife's body. Bewildered and frightened, he trained his eyes on the board, hoping to find some cause as to what had taken her. Shuddering, he let out a whimper when he noticed that the small cross that had been carved through the middle of the board had changed. It had enlarged and gained an airy substance. It was dark, even blacker than the ebony of the board, and its depth was unnatural. He went down on one knee, lowering his head until it was merely inches above the board, and then he peered into the center of the cross.

When he felt the pull, he didn't even have enough time to wonder if he would feel pain.

For the longest time I had this strange scene in my head of a man standing outside during a blizzard—slitting the throat of another man. One evening I decided to write the scene. Like most of the tales I write, I have no idea where the story's going until I start it, and this one was no exception. Once the throat-slashing was done and the character, Robert, was in the bar, the tale took on a life of its own and I was simply along for the ride. Hints of my Catholic upbringing and associated guilt are evident in this work. This story was written recently, and it's published here for the first time.

Something New

Despite the blizzard and the sub-zero temperatures, Robert was surprised by how little time it took to kill the son of a bitch.

The fierce winds from the evening snowstorm had proved to be Robert's ally. Wind gusts screamed like jet exhaust, whipping through alleys and over automobiles, slamming headfirst into the façades of the buildings surrounding him. Its symphony of shrieks and hollow-sounding whispers had covered the crunch of his shoes as he advanced through the snow. He had crept behind the man, grabbed his forehead, and yanked back. A honed knife across the man's throat completed the task.

Had it even registered with the son of a bitch that his throat was cut? The slice was so smooth there was no muscle or tissue resistance. Robert had even questioned it himself as to whether the blade had broken the man's skin. He got his answer moments later when a warm coating bathed his fingers.

Robert loosened his hold on the man. The corpse's knees buckled and the body collapsed face down on the sidewalk. The deep, newly disturbed snow around the body's head turn maroon.

Unmoved, he watched the snow soak up the blood. He alternated his grip on the weapon—loosening and then tightening his fingers around the handle. Blood dripped from the end of the blade, making holes that grew deeper, wider, and darker into the blanket of white that surrounded his legs.

While the wind continued to hammer at him, he went down on one knee, sinking to his mid-thigh in the snow. He wiped the blood off his fingers onto the coat of the dead man, and then did the same with his weapon. Though the frigid air punished his hands, he took his time, and took several swipes with the knife. He turned the blade over each time until it was clean enough to place into his own pocket.

He gazed at the body and could feel his chest tighten with anger. His surroundings faded into the background as he focused on the hatred he had for the man. He clenched his fists, and resisted the urge to repeatedly plunge the knife into the corpse.

Robert slipped the knife into the right pocket of his suit coat and stood. He scanned the area and searched for witnesses or anything out of the ordinary, but the wind whipped the snow around him so forcefully he couldn't see more than a few feet in any direction. He smiled at his good fortune—it was unlikely that he would have been seen by anyone. It was ironic, his getting away with murder was never a consideration. His intent was simple...kill the bastard.

It was time to leave, so he turned his back to the body and retraced his steps. His tracks were filling with snow, vanishing before his eyes. He paused. He had no idea which direction to go.

The wind intensified, so he leaned into it while cold needles peppered his face. His clothing—a suit coat, slacks, and dress shoes—had conspired against him. He was numb, and his thoughts were turning cloudy. He imagined an accumulating crust of snow settling on his eyelids.

Why didn't I prepare for this?

That last thought stayed with Robert. Why hadn't he considered a plan of action succeeding the murder? Why didn't he have an escape route mapped out? How hard would it have been for him to put on a fucking winter coat?

A response took root in the back of his mind. An answer struggled to be heard but as quickly as it had appeared it was gone, suffocated beneath a cold fog of confusion.

In an effort to stay warm, his body had spent the adrenalin generated by the killing. His current condition was proof that he couldn't produce enough body heat to keep the frigid temperature at bay. With his thoughts skewed and his sense of direction non-existent, he bent his head so low that his chin brushed against his chest. Out of desperation he trudged forward. Wind gusts pushed and pulled at him as he made his way. He was unable to judge whether he was walking in a straight line or angling out toward the street. Traveling blind and shivering, if he didn't come to some type of shelter soon, he would be as dead as the man whose throat he had just sliced open.

He lifted his head, forced his eyes open, and focused into the distance. The wind hammered spikes of frozen snow into his eyes, and he thought he could feel the lenses glazing over with frost. Images he'd seen of mountain climbers, dead, sitting with their backs against an ice wall, their eyes permanently frozen open, came to him. Had those men tried to stare down death and lost? A vision of him sitting in the snow, frozen in place, staring into oblivion, formed in his mind. But before it was fully realized, something flashed in front of him, diverting his thoughts.

It was much bigger than a headlight and it flickered in the distance.

Whether it was a rational thought process that drove him or some primordial instinct for survival, Robert responded to the prompt. In a daze, he shuffled toward the light.

He had no memory of the trip or any idea of how long it took for him to make it but he found himself clear-headed, and facing a snow-covered door. He looked for a handle, not finding it, he removed his right hand from his pocket and pushed at the door. It wouldn't open.

Sighing, Robert brushed his hand against the right edge of the door, removing as much snow as he could and found the handle.

He wrapped his frozen fingers around it and pulled. The door opened but only a few inches, catching on the snow at its base. He kicked away the snow along the threshold and pulled the door open enough for him to turn sideways and shimmy inside.

Like a slap in the face, the warmth of the building was unexpected and stung, but Robert welcomed it. He grimaced from the pain as his body thawed. Stomping his feet and rubbing his hands together, he tried to expedite the process. While his limbs were as stiff as rocks, at least they were throbbing—he was thankful that his blood still pumped through them.

Was I out there long enough to have frostbite? The tingling in his toes, fingertips, and cheeks told him otherwise. Another question came to him, *"Why was I even out there in the first place?"*

"Come on inside! Get away from that door! Come over here and get warm!"

Robert heard the command but it sounded so far away he wasn't sure if he had imagined it. He looked to where he thought it originated. Though much of the fog in his brain had dissipated, his vision still gave him trouble. His view was limited, as if he was seeing through a hollow tube, but when he focused, he saw the upper half of a large man, waving him over.

Robert ignored the pain ricocheting through his body, focused on the image, and tried to reconcile why half a man was inviting him in. His vision broadened, and as his surroundings became clearer, he saw that the half-man was standing behind something. A large mirror behind the man came into view, along with shelves filled with bottles of liquor. A number of tables and chairs were scattered throughout the room, and in an alcove off to the side were more shelves stacked with dishes and drinking glasses. He noticed another man sitting on a stool at the far right side of bar. The man, who had not acknowledged him was dressed in winter attire. The man's head was bent low, studying the drink before him. Robert turned from the tavern's sole customer and faced the bartender.

Shaking his head, the bartender looked Robert up and down. Frustrated he asked, "What's the matter? Do I have to come over there and get you?"

Robert took a moment to let the questions settle. Though he had no reason to feel this way, the bartender made him nervous, as did the solitary figure at the end of the bar. His impulse was to slip back through the door, to get as far away from this tavern as possible. Except he didn't relish the thought of going back into the deep-freeze outside. It would be a death sentence. A notion came to him, making him as uncomfortable as heading back out into the storm: *I'm supposed to be here.*

Stomping his feet once more and then brushing the snow off his head and shoulders, Robert gave his body a vigorous shake. "No," he finally answered the bartender, and made his way through the maze of tables and chairs to the bar. He took a seat on one of the stools in front of the big man. Before ordering, he took a few moments to study the bartender. Pantomiming a grin, the bartender shifted his gaze toward the ceiling. He was obviously posing, allowing Robert time for an inspection.

He was even bigger than Robert had initially thought. He had to be around 300 pounds, his upper body more muscle than fat. His pate was naturally bald and so shiny that Robert wondered if the man applied a paste to it. His face was round—almost comically chubby, but the handlebar mustache he wore gave him gravitas. His lips were closed, and Robert could see that they were fleshy—as thick as breakfast sausages. The big man's eyebrows were bulky, bringing to mind bird nests.

Robert lowered his gaze and saw that the bartender's immaculately clean, pressed white shirt clung tightly. Robert marveled at the strength of the seams. Two wide, red suspender straps gripped the bartender's shoulders and were stretched taut over the man's barrel chest. Robert thought the only thing missing was a bowtie. It would have made the bartender a perfect caricature from the Old West.

The bartender had remained patient while being scrutinized, but apparently decided that he had had enough. His head dropped quickly, his faux grin vanished, and his eyes narrowed. In a motion so fast that Robert couldn't react to it, the bartender's head darted forward, closing the distance between the two men. Their noses were now only a foot apart. The big man stared hard, his eyes never leaving Robert's.

Robert flinched and then inched back.

In a gruff but measured tone, the bartender broke the silence. "What are you having?"

Robert was too stunned to answer. *What the hell is this guy's problem?* He took a few moments to regain his composure and replied to the bartender in a timid voice, "Something warm." He then added, "Uh, please?"

After staring at Robert for a few more seconds, the bartender broke character and chuckled. His massive shoulders shook at the effort. "Good," he said with some admiration in his voice. "Something new! That's good! We might be making progress here!" The change in attitude didn't last. The bartender's face turned serious. "If you mean coffee, you're out of luck. We're only serving liquor here this evening."

A huge hand with a rag clutched in its fingers appeared from behind the bar. Robert jumped in his seat as the hand moved toward him. Lowering his arm the bartender smirked, and then wiped a dry area on the bar between them.

"Tell you what…" the bartender started.

Robert thought his tone condescending.

"…let me fix you up a nice scotch, neat," the bartender continued. "That should warm your insides."

Robert mumbled a thanks and let out a small breath as the bartender turned his back to reach for a bottle on the shelf.

While the bartender fixed his drink, Robert turned to look at the man at the end of the bar. He hadn't moved since Robert had first spotted him. He could have been a mannequin. Even from this vantage point, Robert couldn't get a good look at the guy's face. The man's head was bent low, and he wore a knit hat of some kind, pulled low over his brow. A plaid scarf draped over his heavy coat. Robert thought about calling out to him, to get his attention so he would look up, but as he peered at the lone figure a shiver ran down his spine. Something was wrong with the man but he'd be damned if he could figure it out.

His apprehension of the man began to wane, instead, he found himself agitated. *Why is that man just sitting there like a statue? The guy never even lifted his damn head when I came through the door! He hasn't even sipped at his drink!*

"Here you go. Dalmore Twenty-eight. Neat."

Startled at the sound of the bartender's voice, Robert jumped. He turned to the bartender, confused. "Did you say Dalmore Twenty-Eight?"

"Yeah, that's what I said. Dalmore Twenty-eight."

"But-but, that's what I drink," Robert stammered. "How did you know?"

The bartender shook his head at Robert. With an expression that Robert took to be pity, the bartender replied, "Yeah, well, whatever. Just drink up."

Robert eyed his drink. *Could this really be Dalmore 28?* He wrapped his palm around the glass, squeezed his fingers tight, and then brought the drink to his lips. He took a sip. It was Dalmore 28! He took a large swallow.

Savoring the flavor in his throat and the burn in his belly, he lifted the glass and looked at it with appreciation. He turned to the bartender and asked, "But how…?"

The bartender finished Robert's sentence for him. "How did I know you drank Dalmore Twenty-eight? I know a lot about you, Robert."

The glass slipped from Robert's hand. It tumbled to the bar and rolled off the side, the amber liquid leaving a puddle between Robert and the bartender.

"I never told you my name. How do you know my name?"

"As I said, I know quite a bit about you, Robert."

Robert's muscles stiffened and his hands shook. The disquieted feeling he had about the bartender when he had first entered the tavern was nothing compared to how he felt about him now. "What...what do you know about me?"

"For starters," the bartender began, "you're not cold anymore."

It was true. Robert felt warm, as if he had been in this tavern all day. He couldn't remember being cold since he first sat down on the barstool. He brought his hand up to his face. His cheeks had stopped burning, and the throbbing in his limbs was gone. How had he gone from being moments away from freezing to death to feeling perfectly normal in a matter of minutes?

He tried to think this through. Maybe it was true, he didn't feel cold anymore, but what did that prove? If this was the type of information the bartender had on him then there was little reason for him to worry. As for the bartender knowing his name, hell, maybe he'd run into him before. Though he couldn't remember ever being in this tavern, maybe he'd visited it once for lunch with a client or stopped by for a drink after work. That had to be how the bartender also knew he drank Dalmore 28! The tension in Robert's body dissipated. Convinced he had solved the riddle, he prepared to order another scotch.

Before Robert had a chance to order, the bartender snapped his wiping rag into the air, balled it into the palm on one hand, and then proceeded to mop up the spill. The man studied Robert as the rag absorbed the expensive scotch. Moments later, a sad grin summarized the examination. He lowered his gaze and peered down at Robert's waist.

The bartender then spoke as he continued to wipe, "You know what else I know about you, Robert? That knife you got on you? It's in a different pocket than the one you slipped it into when you were out there in the snowstorm."

Robert's spine froze, the numbness traveling up to his neck. Whatever food he had eaten earlier that day, combined with the small amount of scotch he had drunk, gurgled in his gut. He struggled to keep from retching.

Robert was certain that there was a knife in his right coat pocket, but for the life of him he couldn't remember why it was there. He had no idea what to say. In an attempt to appear aloof, he leaned back on the stool, trying to maintain a blank expression. He stared at the bartender's face until it blurred and bled into its surroundings. Robert blinked a few times, seeking time to understand what was going on.

Nonplused, the bartender continued to wipe the bar.

Anger flared in Robert but it was brief, and he was confused as to its origin. When he was able to gather his thoughts, he lowered his head and dropped his hand into the right pocket of his suit coat and searched for the knife. It wasn't there. Dropping his other arm, he slipped his hand into his left pocket. His fingers brushed against the handle.

A jumble of questions flooded Robert, each one beginning with the word 'How'? He gazed back at the bartender as he tried to sort them out, trying to focus on which one to ask first. What broke through the jumble wasn't a question. It was an urge—he wanted to deny he had the knife. But he remembered the bartender had seen him reach down to check on the knife—a denial would have been foolish.

The more he thought about a proper response, the more agitated he became. His fear of the bartender began to ebb. Why should he be worried that the bartender knew he had a knife on him? Lots of guys carried knives. The bartender must have seen the handle sticking up out of the pocket while he was making his way to the bar. Who the hell cares what pocket it was in?

With his confidence returning and his ire rising, Robert leaned forward and made eye contact with the bartender. The parlor tricks were starting to piss him off, and it was time for them to stop. "I don't know what game you're playing," he said to the man, "but...." Robert left the sentence unfinished, hoping that the bartender understood the implication behind his stare.

The bartender stopped wiping. He leaned forward, so close that

Robert could smell the man's breath.

"You're right, asshole" the bartender barked, his face tight with anger, "this is a game. Only it's not mine, it's yours."

Robert was the first to blink. He backed away. His temper remained high, and he fought to control it. He fingered the knife in his pocket. When his fingers wrapped around the handle the bartender's neck stiffened, his shoulders rose with the threat and he inched closer. "Don't even think about it," he said. Robert knew he wouldn't be fast enough to get an edge on him so he released the knife and brought both his hands up to the bar. He held them out in a placating manner. In a low but defiant voice, Robert asked the bartender, "Suppose you tell me what the hell is going on here."

The man behind the bar kept his strong gaze on Robert for a few more seconds, and then the bartender's shoulders relaxed. The intensity in his eyes faded. Sighing, he leaned back and stood tall behind the bar.

"Here's the deal, Robert," the bartender began, "though you didn't invent this game we find ourselves in, your actions have made you the central player. This game is like a puzzle, you have to put pieces together to play it. The problem is you're caught in a loop. You forget you're playing the second you walk out of this tavern. Once you cross that threshold you've lost the game, and you have to play all over again."

"Loop? Puzzle? Game? What the hell are you talking about?"

"A year ago, Robert, on this very day, you were working on a project that demanded long hours at the office. You had worked for weeks on it, late into the evenings. That night was no exception. A bad snowstorm was headed toward the city, and you were concerned you couldn't make it home safely. You called your wife around dinner time, telling her that you were worried about how bad the roads would be so you were going to hole up in a hotel near work. But you changed your mind minutes after the phone call. You felt guilty. You were spending too much time away from her so you decided to leave work early, before the storm got too bad. It was a foolish decision for a few reasons. The storm hit early, and it hit hard. The snow was blinding, the drive slow and treacherous. Though you were shook up from some near-accidents, you did make it home safely."

Robert sat speechless, his mind blank. The bartender's words had not only pushed out all of his anger but also his ability to reason. It took a few moments, but when he replayed the man's story in his head, memories crept in and fleshed his tale out. He remembered being surprised as he pulled into his driveway when there were no lights shining through the front window. He had let himself in, flipped on the light switch, and then removed his London Fog overcoat and gloves to put them on the coat rack. He discovered there was already something hanging from the pegs—another man's coat.

Robert shivered at that last memory. He closed his eyes, willing himself to block it out. When he opened them, he saw the bartender staring at him so intently that Robert thought the man had been peering into his head. As soon as Robert finished the thought, the bartender snickered, then resumed his story, picking up where Robert's memory had left off.

"You were confused when you discovered that coat, then suspicious. You called out your wife's name, your voice low but firm. She didn't respond. You saw there was a light on in the upstairs hallway so you walked to the staircase. You stopped at the bottom and listened. You heard a muffled voice you thought was hers. It was coming from the bedroom. You walked up the stairs, your body tense, your fists opening and closing. You stood outside your bedroom door, and you listened. You could hear her voice but you couldn't make out any words. You reached for the doorknob, twisted it, and then pushed the door open wide. Though the bedroom was dark, there was light shining in from the hallway. You saw your wife on the bed, flat on her back, her legs wrapped around a man's waist." The bartender paused, letting the scene sink into Robert's mind.

Numb, Robert dropped his gaze and stared at the surface of the bar. Visions flashed in his head: his wife's eyes…closed, her face contorted in sexual ecstasy, and a man's ass rising and falling as he pumped into her. He recalled her voice, high-pitched and moaning.

"You flew into a rage, Robert," the bartender continued. "You ran to the bed and tore the man off your wife. He landed on the floor facedown and you kicked him, over and over again. You went for his ribs, his head, and his dick. Anywhere you could do him the most damage. Your wife shouted for you to stop. Instead you turned on her. While you were distracted, her lover managed to slip by you and out of the house."

Robert could see it all happening: the pummeling he gave the man, wanting to kill the son of a bitch, his wife on the bed, crying, trying to cover herself up before he started to beat on her...his hands around her throat, squeezing, shouting at her so forcefully his saliva drenched her face. And then, it came to him that he'd never know who was fucking his wife if he killed her, he loosened his hold and asked who the son of a bitch was.

"You were always a belligerent man, Robert. Flying off the handle, quick to anger, distancing yourself from your friends, family, and co-workers. But those hotheaded tendencies were minor compared to the rage you felt after catching your wife in bed with another man. You came close to killing her. Hate had ignited your veins and nothing could extinguish the malice burning inside you."

When the bartender stopped talking, Robert lifted his head, his eyes ablaze.

The bartender kept his own eyes on Robert while turning his head to the left, to the only other occupant of the tavern.

Robert's head turned also.

"When your wife told you his name, you stared at her in disbelief. You released your grip on her throat, and then backed away, unwilling to accept who it was. You watched her cowering, hands to her throat, gasping for air, and you realized she was telling the truth. Calmly, you walked out of the bedroom, made your way downstairs, and poured yourself a drink. After the third one you went into the kitchen and grabbed a knife. Walking to the front door you heard a thump overhead, then footfalls. Was she phoning the police? Calling her lover? The image of her in bed with another man flashed before your eyes, and the anger you had tried to drown out with alcohol returned. You paused, bringing your hands up to your head in an attempt to control your fury. But it was impossible, you couldn't contain it.

"Screaming, you slashed at the couch, the curtains, the walls. Your wrath intensified with every thrust, every slash. It wasn't enough. There was no satisfaction. He needed to die. Throwing the front door open, you slipped the knife into your suit coat pocket, and then you bolted out into the snowstorm."

Robert rose from his seat, slamming both of his fists onto the bar. Staring at the man at the end of the bar, Robert screamed. "YES! THE FUCKER DESERVED TO DIE!"

Kicking his bar stool aside, Robert turned and leaned into the bartender. He glared at him for a few seconds, then turned back to the man sitting at the end of the bar. Robert spoke forcibly but his tone was distant, as if he were thinking out loud.

"I thought I knew where the son of a bitch was headed. It was here, a tavern that was close to his apartment and only blocks away from my house. This is where I knew he spent his free time. I rushed in and took a quick look around. I didn't see him so I went up to the bartender demanding to know if he was here. The bartender didn't want to give me the information. I could tell he was afraid of me. He should have been. I was pissed off, not dressed right for the weather and covered in snow. I pressed him harder, and when that didn't work, I threatened him. He was so scared of me he finally confirmed that the son of a bitch had been here, but he only had one drink and left minutes earlier after receiving a phone call. I left to track him down. He had to be going to his apartment."

Robert continued to stare at the figure sitting at the end of the bar. The man had not looked up during Robert's recitation of events. Robert's face flushed red, his shoulders shook, and his left hand slipped into his coat pocket. But even with all the events coming back to him, and in spite of the bartender's detailed description and his own memories of what had happened that night, Robert still could not remember the identity of his wife's lover.

With his eyes still fixed on the man, Robert asked the bartender through gritted teeth, "It's him, isn't it?"

Before the bartender could answer, the man stood. With his knit hat pulled down to just above his eyes and his head bent low, he walked toward the front door, going through the motions of someone who could make the trip with his eyes closed. He was dressed warm for the weather—his heavy coat brushed up against the maze of tables as he made his way to the entrance of the tavern. When he reached the door he paused, turned slowly and faced Robert. They made eye contact. The man broke it off and turned back to the door. He pushed it open and walked out into the storm.

"Noooooo!" Robert's voice was loud, fierce. There was no anguish in his denial, nor was there any hint of pain—only hate.

The bartender spoke in a low voice. "Yes, that was him. It was your brother."

Robert closed his eyes as his rage possessed him. When he opened them seconds later, they were full of venom. He reached into his coat pocket and pulled out the knife. He studied the blade, imagining it slicing a deep valley into his brother's throat. He would teach him. Nobody, not even his brother, could get away with fucking his wife.

Holding the knife tight, he turned from the bar to follow his brother's path out the door. He didn't get far. A massive hand grabbed his shoulder, pinning him in place.

"Okay, Robert, you have most of the puzzle pieces now, but there is still one you're missing."

Robert shoved the bartender's hand off of his shoulder. Angry and impatient to follow his prey, he spun toward the big man. "What the hell are you talking about?"

"The game, Robert, the game!" The bartender sighed. He blew out his cheeks and narrowed his eyes in frustration. "You can end this now," he said. "So far it's been played out the same way every time. The minute you step out that door you forget all of this. We're doomed to repeat these last twenty minutes, over and over again, unless you find the capacity inside yourself to forgive."

Robert took a step back from him. "You're nuts."

"Listen to me! You're going to leave this tavern and follow your brother into the storm. You are going to kill him, Robert. What happened after that was something you didn't plan on," continued the bartender. "You froze to death out there."

Robert looked down at the knife in his hand. He studied it for a few seconds, switched it back and forth in his hands, and then he returned his gaze to the bartender. He took another step back and said, "You're fucking crazy." But there was a hesitation in his voice, a lack of conviction, giving the bartender a sense of optimism.

"Good! That's good that you're questioning me! That's also something new! Each time we've gone through this lately you've been a little closer to believing me. Put the knife down. Let's talk this through. Let's end this game and we can all move on."

Robert stared at the bartender for almost a full minute without speaking. Finally he broke the silence. His laugh was loud and dripped with sarcasm.

"You're trying to tell me that I'm in some kind of purgatory, that I'm paying a penance for killing my brother? Who, by the way, WAS FUCKING MY WIFE! And the only way I can atone for this sin is by forgiving him?"

"No," replied the bartender, "that's not what I'm saying."

Robert erupted. He pointed the knife at the bartender, jabbing it into the air while screaming, "THEN WHAT THE FUCK ARE YOU SAYING?"

"I'm not saying that you are in purgatory, Robert. I'm saying that your brother is."

Robert's eyes lost their intensity and he brought the knife down to his side. He turned slightly from the big man. He stood motionless, staring at the floor.

The bartender's voice had a lilt of hope to it. "Forgive him, Robert. He's paid his penance—overpaid in my estimation. Let him move on."

Robert faced the bartender again. His voice was hard, challenging. "And then what? Do I move on, too?"

"Yeah, but I don't know where you move on to. You're a murderer, Robert. It takes more than one person to forgive you."

Much to the bartender's disappointment, a crooked smile appeared on Robert's face. Robert slipped the knife into his right coat pocket and turned to face the door. After a short hesitation, he walked toward the door. He stopped halfway and turned toward the bartender. "I don't believe a word you said, but let's pretend it's true for a moment. What's your angle in all this? You weren't even the man behind the bar when I came in looking for the son of a bitch."

The bartender lifted both of his arms, suspending them above his head, his palms facing out. Robert's eyes narrowed when he saw the sleeves of the bartender's white shirt growing dark. The staining started at his wrists and traveled down past the man's elbows. The bartender brought his hands together and unbuttoned the cuffs on the shirt. He then rolled the sleeves until they bunched at his shoulders. Along the length of his arms were long seeping gashes. Blood bubbled from the incisions.

The bartender stared at Robert. "We all have a penance to pay, Robert. The thing is, unlike you and your brother, I don't know if suicides can be forgiven. All I know is that, so far, I've been destined to help others so they can move on."

Robert, his face devoid of emotion, turned from the bartender and continued to the door. He pushed it open, but paused before going out. With his clothes rippling and his hair flying in the wind, Robert turned to face the bartender.

If the bartender had any hopes that Robert would change his mind, they were dashed. The big man understood all too well when he heard Robert laugh. The results of his efforts would be the same as every other time. Sighing, he dropped his arms. The blood rushing from the cuts ceased and then disappeared, the wounds turning to scars. And as he had done so many times before, he waited.

Robert pushed through the door, plowing his way through the deep snow. He saw fresh tracks, following along with them until he saw a figure in a familiar winter coat.

When he caught up with the man, he was surprised at how little time it took to kill the son of a bitch.

I wrote "Stardust" after reading Mercedes Murdock Yardley's short story collection, Beautiful Sorrows. Her collection contained many of her "star" stories, which were, for the most part, melancholy in tone and quite fantastical. I was captivated by them and longed to use the premise of a falling star as a catalyst for a character's change for the better. (If you've read "Stardust", you may or may not agree if the character's change turned out for the better). I would urge any of my readers to pick up Beautiful Sorrows as it is one of the most enjoyable and satisfying single author collections I have ever read.

I had read "Stardust" last June at Anthocon, an annual genre convention held in Portsmouth, N.H. I mention this for two reasons. The first is I started choking while reading the story and I had a difficult time breathing. Christopher Golden saved my life (well, at the time I thought I was going to die) when he jumped out of his chair and assisted me. The second reason I bring it up is after I finished the reading, authors Bracken McCleod and James A. Moore approached me and expressed how much they enjoyed the story. Jim asked me where he could purchase it and I told him it was not published. He strongly urged me to submit somewhere as soon as I could. When Crossroad Press agreed to publish this collection, my first thought was to let both Bracken and Jim know "Stardust" had found a home.

STARDUST

Despite his years of practice, the blows from my father's fists are delivered onto Meghan without precision or restraint. The kerosene lamp balanced atop a shelf on the wall provides enough illumination for me to witness the welts that form across her cheeks and the swelling of her lips. The remainder of her body will soon be covered in similar bruises. My twin sister's screams are unrelenting and shrill—if they get any sharper my ears will bleed.

I have no clue as to what prompted this latest beating, though I am sure that it would be considered, at worst, a misdemeanor by any reasonable family court. No matter, any infraction perceived by our father had always led to cruel and, as I'd learned judging from anyone else's standards, unusual punishment. Having no choice, lest I risk sharing my sister's plight, I escape her high-pitched wails by sneaking out of the house and venturing into the night.

Wearing only evening dress, I tread lightly and barefoot past the dusty portrait of President Roosevelt hanging crookedly in our dining parlor, fleeing out the front door and onto our porch's rickety steps. Lifting my heels, I tiptoe over boards warped from the rain and splintered from the heat of the sun. I pray all the while their groans of protest will be covered by the sounds of my sister's agony. Reaching the bottom step without consequence, I rush into the darkness.

The night has always been my refuge.

My evening retreat is a hastily constructed berm located a good distance from our house that partitions our property from the entrance to a cornfield. The weed- and shrub-choked cornfield hasn't been farmed since our mother passed on ten years ago. While no notices were posted, nor was it ever spoken of in our house, I assumed that the town had claimed it from our family due to arrears.

Crabgrass also claimed the berm as its own. The invasive weed grew wild and tall over the mound, serving as a sometimes prickly yet adequate cushion for those times when I lay on my back to gaze at the night sky.

In my haste, I had forgotten about my lack of footwear as I sped from the house to the berm. The abundance of ragged stones, broken twigs, and rusted scraps of metal that littered my path must all have had some premonition of my arrival as they have aligned themselves in such a way as to do the most damage to my feet.

Reaching the berm, I lower myself into the crabgrass, sighing as it envelopes me. Blood oozes from my soles, nourishing their roots. Ignoring the pain, I lie down and close my eyes, dreaming of things visible, yet out of reach.

When I was younger, I had a teacher in the higher-education classes who took note of my interest in the things celestial. He took pity on me and schooled me in the nature of stars and the study of constellations. I discovered only after our extra-curricular sessions had begun that he had wanted to advance much more toward me than the knowledge of the heavens. I came to accept both his intellectual teachings and the physical ones. By the time my father had pulled me from school to assist on the farm, I considered myself learned in the art of literature, astronomy, and of earthly pleasures.

Pushing aside these memories, I open my eyes wide and see that the night sky is exceptionally clear. I am having no trouble locating the outlines of my favorite constellations. Taurus is easily visible, as is Orion directly below it. I search for the Pleiades, and having found it, I can make out the six stars that can be seen without a telescope. But something about the Pleiades is odd. There is a seventh star visible in the cluster, brighter than the others. It is heavily tinted with gold—not the white hue in which we most commonly view stars. This by itself would make the apparition odd, but I also notice that it is much larger than any other star in the sky. Even stranger, the star is in motion.

The pain in the soles of my feet forgotten, I stand to look closer at the star. It has to be an optical illusion or a flight of fancy, but as I stare at the unfamiliar bright star, it appears to be hurtling in my direction. As its proximity to me shortens, conversely, its intensity heightens—it looks ablaze! It glows so much I imagine it vomited from the sun, leaving a contrail of flaming diamond-like embers in its wake as it streaks toward me.

It occurs to me I must be witnessing a meteor falling to earth, but I dismiss the notion when I notice the size of the star remains constant. This makes no sense. My eyes must be playing tricks, but after rubbing them and looking up again, the size of the star has not changed. If anything, it is more luminescent. As I gaze at the star, never once do I entertain the urge to flee or panic as I watch it approach.

Fingers of flame discharge from the star as it breaches our atmosphere, and it continues on a determined path toward me, plunging through the night sky like a flaming Icarus. Minutes later, it crashes to the earth, no more than a mere ten feet away from me. My interest toward it is so great that I do not as much as flinch upon its impact. Instead, I climb off of the berm and approach the spot where it made contact with the ground. As I stand over it and study the fallen star, my incredulity finally prompts an emotional response—I gasp in wonder at the sight.

The star looks exactly as a child would see in a play book. It resembles the stars on an American flag with its smooth outline and five digits that radiate out to points. It was approximately three feet wide between its opposing tips, and its color is as gold as the decorative trim on my mother's teacups. And, it glows so brightly! Oddly, I feel no heat radiating from the star, and I notice that the ground surrounding it is not parched.

In the recess of my mind, warnings are taking root. There is no doubt this is an unnatural occurrence, defying not only the laws of physics, but the dictates of logic and common sense. Still, I brush aside the negative portents and kneel close to the object to study it further. I have an overwhelming urge to touch it. There is no indication that touching the star would result in any harm to me. I reach out and brush my fingertips against its surface. It is coated with a fine dust. *Stardust,* I imagine with a smile as my fingers create small canals through it.

My smile lasts no more than a few seconds.

A gelatinous mass of stardust, as molten as any iron ore poured from a kettle in a foundry, slithers up from its surface and onto my fingertips. It crawls over my fingers, past the first and then the second set of knuckles until it takes complete possession of my hand. I attempt to pull away, but my hand holds fast. Though I have not yet felt any pain I cringe, and wait for the inevitable.

It never comes.

I take a deep breath and stare at my hand. The stardust, intense as a bolt of lightning, travels along the length of my arm. I am puzzled it causes no injury. Actually, the opposite is true—I am invigorated.

The stardust burns through my evening dress, attaching itself to me, absorbing my flesh unto itself. I sense a consciousness to the stardust. Its essence is remarkably powerful, delivering a constant flow of energy through my nerves, my muscles, and my mind. I am aglow wherever the stardust passes over me, luminescence radiates in every direction. I derive remarkable strength from it, and I derive a certain knowledge from the stardust—a knowledge that I am capable of much more than I ever had been.

I had been weak all of my life, unsure, eager to please. Vermin have terrified me and insects have caused me panic. I have been afraid of threats from authority, the sight of a man's belt in his hand, the visage of a closed fist, and lust derived from the sight of my flesh through the bottom of a bottle. No more.

The stardust has completely enveloped me. I am a human torch. I lift my hand from the star and swing my arms. I am amazed at how they blaze, how they leave contrails of flaming diamond-like embers in their wake. I have been made new by an omnificent star, and I am now prepared to make my own destiny.

As I return to our home, I look behind me. I expect to see flaming footprints burned onto the grass, but there are none. For this I am grateful, as I have no desire to burn down the house.

Standing in front of the house, I listen. There are no screams of pain or any moans that I can discern. My sister's punishment must be over. From experience, I imagine her cowering in bed with thin sheets pulled up tightly over her head while the pillow sops her tears. I take the front steps one at a time, making a silent vow that this night will be the last of our suffering from our father's hand. I push open the door and stride into the parlor, illuminating even the darkest corners as my determination fuels the stardust within me.

To my surprise, I see both my father and sister are in the parlor. Meghan is bent forward at the hip over the dining table with her petite breasts flattened against its surface. Her hands are extended, fingers gripping the far edge of the table. Her night dress is lifted and bunched around her midriff. I can see the results of my father's punishment on her lower back and legs. Her head is angled toward me but her eyes are closed. She is unable to acknowledge my presence, I cannot tell if this is because she has withdrawn inside herself from the assault or if she has passed out from it.

The notion occurs to me that someone not familiar with our circumstances might mistake a look of satisfaction adorning my sister's face.

I know different.

Our father is sitting on a wooden dining room chair a short distance away from Meghan. The chair is turned to the wall and his back is to me. All I can see of him is the top of his shoulders and a balding head of brittle gray hair dotted with liver spots. I also notice an empty bottle of bourbon, and the belt from his pants in the space separating us. I take a step toward him, but hesitate when he speaks.

"You're back."

His speech is slurred, the words run together. He does not turn around to address me and it makes me furious. I burn brighter, bathing the parlor in light so bright that I fear it would burn my sister's eyes if she opens them. I did not speak, but wait for him to turn to me in wonder, and fear. Finally, he rises from the chair, turns, and faces me.

I am confused. His face displays no fright, and his eyes do not narrow in the presence of my illumination. His stance, though wobbly from drink, betrays no reaction from my threatening appearance. He stares at me for a moment with his head cocked to one side. He straightens his head and addresses me.

"You look different somehow, and what happened to your night clothes?" He says these things casually, as though he's speaking to the person I once was. Then, his eyes light up as if some great truth has occurred to him. "You want your turn, don't you?" He laughs at his revelation.

How can this be? Can he not see what I have become? I look at my body and I am still burning, but not as bright. Anxiety floods through me. Is my father's control over me so complete that he can extinguish a fire that burns so intense? Doubt worms its way through me, and I tremble. Once again, I am feeling weak, overwhelmed, and I long for assurance. Then, an idea occurs to me.

I turn to look at Meghan. I rush to her side and bend awkwardly over her. I am not certain that I won't burn her so I am reluctant to lay my hands upon her. Instead, I lean close to her ear and whisper her name. There is no reaction, so I whisper it again. She doesn't move. I have to make my decision quickly, but I pause before doing so. I think back on my actions since leaving the berm and entering the house. I remember the grass was untouched after I had stepped on it. I look around me and see there are no flames eating the wood.

I won't hurt her!

Carefully, I lower my hands and place my palms on the sides of her body. Her gown does not burst into flames nor blacken from my touch. Relief washes over me. Reaching out, I remove her fingers from the edge of the table and then I turn her over so she is on her back. Though my hands are aflame, I have no fear of injuring her, so I gently caress her face and call to her. Thank God! There is a reaction.

Meghan stirs, and then opens her eyes to me. She squints and blinks as she comes around. She freezes when her eyes lock on mine. Her face then tightens and her mouth opens so wide I can see her tongue retracting. Panic paints her features, and she recoils from me. I am emboldened by her reaction. I understand her fear. She is afraid of being burned! I hold her shoulders so she won't slip away, and I lean closer to her. Her hands move from her sides, and she shields her eyes from my brilliance. She has not spoken a word, so I break the silence.

"Never again," I say to her shaking my head. I remove my hands from her and she slides off the table and rolls beneath it. She cowers there, waiting for what happens next.

Her wait is not long.

I turn to face my father. His eyes are shining, and he is grinning.

"It's your turn now," he mumbles and breathes heavily. Leaning over to retrieve the belt, he demands, "Come to Daddy, boy."

I stare back at him. Aside from what I am to do, my mind is clear. There is no fear of punishment—there is no fear of pain. Though he does not register it, the stardust inside me burns brighter than before. I can feel the house cleansing. The color surrounding me bleeds to white.

I turn away from him and approach the edge of the table. I bend over it in the position in which I found my sister when I re-entered the house. I reach out and wrap my fingers over the far edge, and then I spread my feet apart. I can hear his footsteps as he approaches, and when they stop, he is standing behind me.

He grunts as he swings the belt.

I laugh when the buckle strikes flesh.

When he tires, there is a pause—I know what is to come next. I push away from the table and slam against him. My father swears aloud at the contact, and he takes a few unbalanced steps backward. When I turn around to face him, I see he is on fire. There is shock on his face as he looks down upon himself. I do not give him the opportunity to dwell on it.

I rush toward him, wrapping both my blazing hands around his neck and squeeze. The stardust flows from my fingers like lava and it envelopes him. His flesh melts, it drips over his corpulent belly. My hands sink deeper and his arms flail uselessly at me. His eyes bulge and his mouth contorts into an obscene grimace, and then he slips toward the floor. He is dead weight, but I will not let him go. Squeezing tighter, I stare into his wide eyes and nod when his head bursts into flames. I let him fall—his body makes a dull thump as it hits the floor. Satisfied, I watch his head burn until it is nothing but ash. When it is over, when the fire is out and the last curl of smoke rises and vanishes, I leave him and go to my sister.

From the look on her face, there is no doubt she has watched as I murdered our father. Her eyes are wide and though she is looking in my direction, she is staring through me. She does not make a sound, but she is trembling.

"Don't be afraid," I tell her, "give me your hand, I will not burn you."

Meghan reaches out to me. I take her hand and fold it into mine. She relaxes, and her hand turns limp. Holding onto it firmly, I pull her out from under the table.

"I can control it," I explain to her when she stands upright. "I will not burn you."

She has calmed down, the trembling has stopped, and she is gazing at me with a blank expression that I take to be a mixture of curiosity and wonder.

"I am remade," I continue. "A star in the night fell and I have absorbed the power within it. I burn with strength and knowledge now, and I have a new destiny to fulfill. I am stardust. You can be like me, Meghan. Twenty-six years ago our mother gave birth to us, now we will both be reborn."

It took her a few moments to nod her response.

I lead Meghan to her bedroom, and I share with her the gift of stardust. She smiles. She glows. She burns as brightly as I do.

She slips off of the bed, and then, holding hands, we walk through the parlor to the front door and descend the front steps. When we reach the ground, we look to the night sky. We smile, knowing that we are their brethren.

We are golden.

We are stardust.

This story came about from another prompt, this time from my writers group. Cat Pragoff, our moderator at the time, threw out a few lines about flowers thrown over a gravesite and asked us to write a story around those lines. The premise came to me quickly, but I was uncertain of the result having never served our country in war. "The Soldier's Wife", was picked up by Anthology-Year Two, with Johnny Morse, the editor, telling me his first read was enough to accept it. Several months after it was published, I had read a review on the anthology. The review mentioned my story, and it removed any uncertainties I had over the work.

THE SOLDIER'S WIFE

A pained smile etched Claudine's face as her fingers lingered on the small box in her pocket.

She supposed that if her father-in-law had been gazing her way he surely would have mistaken her facial expression for a frown. With the corners of her mouth pulled back and the worry lines on her cheeks so prominent, only a close look into her eyes would have given him any clue to the contrary.

"I'm sorry, Claudine, you deserved better," he murmured through barely parted lips as he stood before his son's grave. His stiff posture and his drooping head made him appear as if he was staring at his shoes.

"Frank..." began Claudine, but she had barely gotten his name out before he interrupted.

"He was a shit to you!" His voice tinged with restrained anger. "He couldn't provide a decent home or even hold a job long enough to feed the both of you, but he had no problem finding the cash to buy booze or drugs, though, did he? How many times did he come home late stinking of cheap whiskey or so high he couldn't even make it to his bed, Claudine? How many times did he even bother to come home at all? And when he did come stumbling in late at night, what about the arguments, the fights?"

He made a point of looking disgustedly at the bruises around her neck.

She shrugged him off. "He had his problems Frank, I know that, but he loved me and he was faithful."

Frank's face turned a deep shade of red and his voice rose. "The only thing he was faithful to was a bottle or those drugs he took! He didn't give a crap about you, me, or anyone else. When did he ever go out of his way and put that damned bottle down or say no to a drug dealer? When did he do a single good deed for another human being? Look around you, Claudine! We're the only two people who bothered to come to your husband's funeral."

She sighed as Frank turned from her and looked back toward the grave. He focused on the small flat stone that simply bore her husband's rank, name, and two dates. Again, he hung his head, burying himself in thought.

Claudine continued to run her fingers over the small box in her pocket. The exterior of the box was covered with deep purple velvet and was stamped with a U.S. Marines' insigne. Inside was a medal, a Silver Star for bravery. Her husband had been awarded the medal for having saved eight men who had been ambushed on a routine patrol mission in Afghanistan, with disregard for his own life. On the very day of his return home from duty, her husband had casually tossed the medal on top of a bureau and remarked that he had refused to attend the award ceremony. They had sent the medal to him anyway. He had also told her that he would have gladly given it back in exchange for the ten lives he hadn't saved in that ambush. He hadn't touched the medal since then, nor had he ever spoken of it.

Their relationship had been strained since his return from the war; her husband having suffered terribly for his heroics. The emotional abuse toward her had started early, and occasionally, it had become physical. She'd borne the insults and the drunken violence, understanding their source. She knew he still loved her; their crying jags left no doubt in her mind. So she had willingly shared his burden, knowing the day would come when he sought help, and things would be as they were before he had enlisted. He was a hero, and she loved him all the more for it.

After a few minutes, Frank walked limply away from his son's gravesite. With his shoulders sagged in defeat, Claudine thought he looked much older than a man in his early fifties. He stopped several yards away and leaned heavily on a headstone. Claudine barely heard him as he spoke, "Only two of us to send that poor excuse for a son away."

She was ready to go home, content to leave the old man ignorant about his son, and to let him wallow in his misery.

When she turned from Frank to begin the trip back to the car, she stopped short. There was a haze of some sort, a fog-like substance swirling in the air a short distance before her. As she stared, the haze grew denser, and she thought she could make out shapes within it. Her eyes must have been playing tricks, she reasoned, so she rubbed them with both hands and then looked back. In the few seconds it took to rub the disbelief from her eyes, the shapes had taken ghostly but distinct forms. Claudine gasped.

Before her stood the shades of ten men in service uniforms, their visage like waves of heat rising from a sun-burnt blacktop. They were smiling, wholly formed, and walking toward her husband's gravesite in formation. When they arrived, they broke rank and formed a broad circle around the grave. They stood there, rigid and unmoving, all of them gazing at the flat stone. As if a silent signal had been transmitted, they all went to their knees, and in unison, ten hands reached down and disappeared into the dirt. When their hands withdrew moments later, an eleventh hand could be seen floating up through the ground, clinging tightly to the others. They pulled Claudine's husband up, and he now stood with the ten, grinning and looking as handsome as he ever had. The ten welcomed him as only brothers could.

Claudine smiled. A warm feeling, centered in her chest, began to spread throughout her body. However, as she continued to view the scene playing out before her, something made her pause. Something didn't feel right. Her smile began to falter when she discovered what it was; there was a subtle change occurring on the men's faces. She noticed their smiles turning harder, their eyes narrowing. She blinked rapidly in confusion, unsure of what she was seeing. She focused, squinting at their hazy forms, and she noticed that their spectral hands, so welcoming only seconds earlier, were now curled into closed fists.

The ten servicemen began to move closer to each other, tightening the circle around her husband. She watched as his grin faded, confusion clouding his features. Soon, a look of panic overtook him. A chill worked its way up her spine when she saw his fear.

In a fury, they descended on him.

With unrelenting precision, the dead servicemen savagely raked and pummeled her husband's ghostly form. They tore the limbs from his body. From the empty sockets, wispy streams of pearl-colored fluid spurt through the air. Claudine thought her husband's pain couldn't have been any worse, but when his arms and legs drifted back toward his body and then reattached themselves, she knew she was wrong. The scene repeated itself as the men inflicted the same damage on him.

Claudine continued to gape at the carnage silently. When some of the men plunged their hands into her husband's stomach, forcibly ripping it open, she stopped breathing. When his vapory intestines tumbled freely to the ground, her head began to swim. Bile rose into her throat when his entrails floated back up into the cavity and the wound resealed itself. Even in a daze, she noticed that the soldiers seemed to delight in their ability to disembowel her husband, over and over again.

Claudine swayed in place and took deep breaths. She had never contemplated whether the dead could feel pain, but if she had, the answer was plainly spelled out before her. Her husband's agony was obvious and intense. Teetering, she watched as the men continued to torture him. And when a hand rested on her shoulder, Claudine jumped and screamed. Turning, she saw Frank standing behind her. He appeared surprised by her fright.

"You know," he said in a solemn voice, "I'm not sure that he ever told you that the Marine Corps presented him with a Silver Star for bravery."

Claudine stared at Frank. How could he stand there talking to her so calmly? Was he really oblivious to what his son was going through or was she the only one who could see it? She wanted to point at the gravesite, force him to gaze at the atrocities that were committed against his son, but she knew it was futile. If it was meant to be, he would have seen what was occurring. The idea that she was being punished came to her. Frank continued to talk, taking no notice of her emotional state. His repeated mentions of the medal finally had an effect on her. For some reason it grounded her, distracting her from her husband's plight. She listened to him, managing an occasional nod, encouraging him to continue with his story.

"To tell you the truth," Frank continued, "I was stunned when they contacted me and sent me a copy of the letter, more so when I found out he had refused to attend the ceremony. It didn't make much sense to them or to me. Why did he refuse to go? So I tracked down those eight men he saved; I wanted to find out what happened firsthand. I did some research, and it wasn't that hard to find them all once I found the first one. Seven of the eight told me the same story, how he was out on point and rushed back to save them when they were ambushed. They said they owed him their lives. But one man, a soldier named Ben, told me a different tale.

"Ben said that he was with your husband on the day of the ambush. They were both snipers, sent out in advance of the company to check for Taliban. They had gone some distance when they came across a young woman, bound to a tree and beaten, probably taken from one of the local villages during a raid. She was still alive, but barely. Your husband decided to take advantage of the situation. Ben argued with him, told him to leave the woman alone, that it could be a ruse, but your husband wouldn't listen. Ben then said that your husband reached into his backpack, took out some white powder and sniffed it. After waiting a moment, he approached the woman.

"Wanting no part of it, Ben walked back to his company and was caught in the ambush. They were pinned down for almost twenty minutes, a lifetime for all of those men, and an end to their lives for some. Ben was badly wounded, unconscious when your husband finally came back and returned fire. At the hospital, Ben was told about how your husband came back from patrol and saved the rest of the men, but he never said a word to anyone about why your husband took so long."

Claudine found herself distancing her hand from the medal that sat in her pocket.

"His fellow servicemen, most of them his friends, were killed while he was high on coke and raping a helpless woman. That's why he didn't want to attend the medal ceremony, Claudine. It had nothing to do with grief or being humble. What little conscience he had made him realize how guilty he was for the ones who had died. That medal would always be a constant reminder of how repugnant he was."

Claudine turned from Frank and looked back at the gravesite. The ten men continued their assault on her husband. If anything, it looked as if the beating had intensified.

"After listening to Ben's story I debated whether to tell you," Frank went on, "but I decided against it. You wouldn't have believed me anyway. Spiritually, you're just like him. You've let him get away with his selfish and destructive acts ever since he returned from Afghanistan, and that makes you not only complicit with what he was, but just as reprehensible."

Claudine shifted, leaning back at his words, stunned, but unable to refute them.

"I prayed to God every night since he returned, Claudine. I prayed that he would pay for his acts, especially the one in Afghanistan. But God never answered those prayers— until now, I guess." Frank removed his hand from her shoulder and walked away slowly.

After following him with her eyes until he was out of sight, Claudine turned back to the gravesite. Though the men continued their attack on her husband, their shades were less substantial; they were fading. Unable to look away, she watched them maul her husband until all of their foggy substance had completely vanished. Then, with her head hanging low, she took small steps over to the gravesite.

Claudine looked down on the freshly packed soil, not knowing what to expect. Would she see her husband's agonized face staring back at her? Would the ten servicemen who lost their lives due to her husband's destructive ways stare back at her in pity? Would they reach up and exact their vengeance on her as well? She folded her knees and bent low, extending a clenched hand until it touched the ground. She opened her hand and then pulled it back. A small, purple velvet box now rested on the flat stone.

"I'm sorry," she said, not knowing whom she was addressing, "I am so sorry."

This might be the most ball-breaking story I have ever written. My wife is a Born Again Christian so I am exposed to the occasional sermon concerning my evil ways and the positive power of prayer. As I've discovered, it's impossible to reason with a Born Again Christian so I decided to write a story challenging the tenants of faith rather than getting into a no-win argument with her.

When I finished the first draft, I presented it to my writers group. One member called the story blasphemous and she refused to finish reading it. I explained to her the story was actually faith affirming but she refused to believe it (she later left the group). One of our members is a Catholic priest, Father John, and his comments were very encouraging.

I believed in the story and continued to revise it. I asked an author friend to look at it but he was not complimentary. I asked others to read it and I received neutral comments, as well as two helpful responses from author's Keith Minnion and Chris Irvin concerning its structure. I worked on it some more. When Tim Deal, the editor for Anthology-Year 3 called for submissions, I sent "Tsunami" to him. I was proud to be in the first two Anthology-Year volumes and I desperately wanted to be included in the third.

Tim read it, and then he did something extraordinary for me. He told me he loved the story, it was original and a page-turner, but I was leading the readers by the hand. He said the readers would understand the plot and sub-text without all the explanation. He gave me five days to work on it before he made a decision.

I rewrote and edited like a madman. I sent the revised story to Sandi Bixler, a member of my writers group, for her opinion. She gave me the thumbs-up and I sent "Tsunami" back to Tim. Hours later, he wrote me back saying it was terrific and he accepted it. Months later, when I attended Anthocon 2015, I ran into Tim Deal in the hallway. It was late at night, and let's just say we were both having a good time at the convention. He stopped, looked me straight in the eye, and said, "Tsunami. Wow." Then, he kept on walking.

TSUNAMI

A sense of unease weighed on Emily as she stared out over the ocean. The atmosphere on the beach had changed, turning oppressive. A slight breeze cooled her sun-broiled skin. For the life of her, she couldn't figure out why she felt so unnerved, and no matter how hard she tried, she couldn't shrug it off. Reaching up, she caressed the small gold cross hanging from her neck.

She glanced over at her husband Carl, who was building sandcastles with her son. While her thirteen-year-old, Stephen, enjoyed the sculpting and the playful banter with his father, her youngest, Samantha, sat a few feet away from them scooping up fistfuls of sand and letting it flow through her fingers. At seven years old, Samantha was a mischievous child, a free spirit who possessed the curiosity of a feline and questioned everything, endlessly it seemed. Emily kept an eye on her; there was no telling if Samantha would wander off and get too close to the shoreline.

The island they were vacationing on was not large or commercialized, which was what attracted them to it in the first place. It didn't offer many amenities other than a decent hotel and a first-class beach located in a small, private cove surrounded with palm trees. There weren't a lot of tourists on the island, which left Emily and her family plenty of space to play and relax. The beach itself was spectacular with the cleanest white sand she had ever seen buffering the hotel from the ocean. The saltwater was sparkling clear with only a touch of cobalt—appearing as fresh as any pond or lake back home in the mountains of New Hampshire. Best of all, the water was pleasantly warm and refreshing, a far cry from the freezing temperatures they had left behind.

Samantha stopped playing and rose to her feet. After a few moments of twirling and imitating the seagulls that flew overhead, she walked over to her father and brother. While they tried to involve her in the construction of their castle, Samantha wanted no part of it. Instead, she moved a few feet from them, stopped, and then looked out over the ocean.

Then, just as Emily had feared, Samantha began to saunter toward the shoreline. Emily was on her feet in seconds, chasing after her daughter. Samantha was quick though, and she was already into the water up to her knees before Emily could get to her.

Reaching her, Emily scooped Samantha up with one arm, preventing her daughter from wading any deeper. But Emily's forward momentum prevented her from coming to a complete stop and she lost her balance, causing both of them to tumble into the surf. Emily's head brushed the sand when they went under. There, a large shard of glass from a broken bottle jutted up from the ocean's floor, filling Emily's vision. She stood quickly, hefting Samantha and holding onto her tight. She silently thanked God that neither she nor Samantha had landed on the glass. Walking back to the beach, she swept the thin blonde hair out of her daughter's eyes. She seemed none-the-worse from the experience and Emily kissed her forehead. "What's the matter, honey? You don't want to play with Stephen and your dad?"

"No, Mommy. I want to play with that woman." Samantha lifted her finger and pointed to the sea.

Emily followed Samantha's gaze.

"Honey, it's probably a boat or a dolphin..." she began, but froze when her eyes caught sight of a figure in the distance. At first glance, it did appear to be a woman and, oddly, it looked as if she were standing upright on the surface of the water.

Indeed, it was a woman, nude, her hair dark, wet, and long enough to cling to her waist. Even from a distance, she could see that the woman's breasts hung heavily from her chest. Emily's focus went to the bottom half of the woman. She concentrated on the woman's feet.

She has to be standing on something!

"Can I play with her Mommy?"

Emily was about to give Samantha a hastily thought-out "no", when her daughter's eyes suddenly went wide. Samantha once again pointed at the woman and then said, "Oh—look!"

Beneath the woman, a wide column of water lifted her skyward.

Emily stared, her mouth agape. From where she stood, the column appeared to be round, at least twice the diameter of the woman and its surface as smooth as ice. The water at the base was undisturbed. There was no spray from the small waves as they collided with the column. It was as if the ocean were diverting around it. Emily wrapped both her arms around Samantha as the column rose, lifting the woman up further into the air. For a brief moment Emily had the impression that the woman was falling, but then she realized that the column had stopped rising. The woman did not react to the cessation of movement and remained still. She looked down upon Emily and Samantha.

Emily turned toward her husband. He and Stephen were absorbed in their work, neither of them aware of what was occurring offshore. She swept her gaze beyond them and across the beach. The other tourists were continuing about their business of sunbathing and chasing their children. She couldn't count one person who was looking out over the water in shock or amazement.

Were they the only ones who could see the woman and that gigantic column of water?

An urge to shout overcame Emily, to get Carl to look toward the sea. With Samantha still tight in her arms, she turned back to face the ocean. When she saw what was happening, she thought she was hallucinating.

In the brief time she had looked away, the column had widened. It was now a huge wall of water, as wide as the entire beach was long. At its ends, the wall veered in, bracketing the beach at ninety-degree angles. Behind Emily, all had gone quiet. The adults, the children, even the seabirds were silent and they all stared in wonder at the ocean. Carl and Stephen stood looking out over the water, her son pointing at the wall with a look of amazement while her husband had turned toward her in fear. Their eyes met and a chill ran though her body. She wanted to reach out to Carl, to hold him for what she intuitively knew would be the last time, but a strong compulsion to face her fear overcame her. She turned from her husband toward the ocean. Focusing on the woman, Emily immediately regretted her decision.

Below the woman, large gouts of water, resembling solid tubes, exploded out from the length of the wall. The tubes, too many to count, were as wide as boulders and racing through the air, and they were headed toward the beach.

Emily turned away in a panic, cradling Samantha and throwing herself to the sand. Lifting her head, she managed a single sob as she watched her husband and son crushed beneath one of the tubes of water. They were gone in an instant, washed away in the unrelenting tide of water that followed.

The tubes reached them all—men, women, their children, hammered into the beach sand, and then swept away. Emily braced herself, praying that her body would provide enough of a cushion to spare Samantha a crushing death.

The tube of water that came for them somehow missed its target, making contact with the beach a few feet before them. The sand beneath them shook, and then less than a second later the tide swept them forward.

Emily struggled to grip Samantha as they propelled through the water. She had a tight hold on both of her daughter's arms but she could feel Samantha slipping away. Something was tugging at her daughter, trying hard to loosen Samantha from her hold. With every tug Samantha slipped further down Emily's arm until, with a strong yank, Samantha was ripped from her grasp. Emily screamed, and seawater rushed in between her parted lips.

Reflexes kicked in, and Emily gagged from the water that she had swallowed. Stomach heaves assaulted her body, and she found herself spasming. She fought hard against it, trying to keep herself from expelling what little air remained in her lungs. She willed her legs to kick, to try to lift herself to the surface, but the current was too strong.

Nearly out of air, Emily stopped struggling to save as much oxygen as possible. After gagging a few more times, the convulsions subsided, and she found herself drifting along with the current. An overwhelming feeling of calmness descended upon her, and the rapid sensation of being pushed forward in the water diminished to the point she thought she was barely moving. She tried to focus, desperate for one last look to find Samantha.

Emily wished that she had simply closed her eyes and let her mind drift away into the darkness.

Bodies, with their heads bowed and their arms hanging uselessly in front of them, spun leisurely in the water around her. The dead were everywhere, in a macabre dance as they drifted and then bounced off each other in slow motion. Most were seriously injured, from missing limbs to severe lacerations. Blood, still oozing from their wounds, created small, puffy, and red-tinted clouds that slowly dissolved in the water. When the gentle current turned the bodies, exposing their faces to her, Emily cringed. Most of their facial features were beaten to pulp. Eyes were missing, noses flattened, and pieces of bone could be seen jutting through their flesh.

Before the water could claim her, she came to a sudden stop—a pressure against her back, something solid, unyielding, holding her in place. Moving her hand to her back, she realized it was the trunk of a palm tree.

Gathering reserves she hadn't realized she still possessed, she wrapped her hands around the trunk and began to pull herself up, forcing herself to climb.

When she broke the surface of the water, the air racing into her lungs hit her like a sledgehammer and her chest erupted in pain. A coughing fit followed but she held on to the trunk. When her body settled enough to where she had control over it, she put her forehead against the palm's rough bark and relaxed. After a few minutes of rest, she lifted her head and gazed past the palm tree.

A short distance away stood a series of buildings. She recognized them as part of the resort, but oddly, her view was skewed. For some reason, she was looking down on the buildings.

The resort had not suffered any damage from the tubes nor did it look as if the tidal waters had reached it. She noticed people—staff from the look of their uniforms—all gathered at the front of the hotel and pointing up in her direction. None of them made a move toward her or the beach.

Why is the resort so far down, and why are they all pointing at me?

After lowering her head slightly, Emily gasped. Only a few feet beyond her, the ocean ended abruptly, vanishing into thin air.

In a panic, she clung so tightly to the palm tree that the muscles in her arms began to lock up. When she was convinced her hold was secure enough to prevent her from drifting off to the edge, Emily turned her head around, to look back at where the beach had been. She saw nothing but a flat expanse of ocean. It was as if the wall of water had come ashore and then run up against an invisible barrier.

Emily maneuvered herself around the palm tree to get a better look. When she settled on the other side, her back now to the resort, she poked her head around the trunk of the tree. She gasped at the site.

Emily was on top of what looked like a gigantic fish tank.

Gazing out over the water, she noticed that many of the dead were floating on the surface. Thoughts of Carl, Stephen, and Samantha stabbed at her heart, and her tears mingled with the seawater.

A movement around one of the bodies closer to Emily caught her eye. It was a man, belly up with his arms stretched wide. His body bobbed a few times, and then it was gone, pulled down into the depths. She watched as, one by one, the same thing happened to other bodies. Sobbing, she waited for whatever was in the water to reach her.

Small waves brushed up along Emily's right side. They weren't powerful, but they were strong enough to catch her attention. She turned in their direction. Ten feet away the seawater boiled. Dozens of large bubbles were pushing their way up through the water and then bursting when they made contact with the air. Something was coming from below. When it broke through, Emily could only stare.

A woman was rising out of the water. Her features were bloated, her skin tinted blue. Small sections of her body were missing, including most of her fingers and toes. The woman continued to rise until the soles of her feet were even with the surface. She stared at Emily, her eyes milky and bulging from their sockets.

At the sight of the woman Emily wanted to let go of the tree trunk and swim away, but her hands refused to let go. Her heartbeat accelerated and she began to tremble violently. A scream fought its way up her throat, but before she could take a deep enough breath to expel it, her head grew heavy and her mind clouded over. Her heart rate slowed and her shaking subsided.

This muddled feeling lasted only a few more moments before it vanished as quickly as it had come. She began thinking clearly again and, oddly, she found herself less fearful of the woman. Emily faced her, staring deeply into the woman's opaque eyes.

"You survived."

The words were not spoken aloud but had appeared in Emily's head.

The woman approached Emily, gliding inches above the surface and stopping a few feet before her. An image of Jesus walking on the water flashed into Emily's mind.

"Ah, the man called Jesus," the woman noted. "I have seen the image of this man several times in your people's minds, but this is the first I have seen it associated with traveling over water. He is usually thought of in the moments associated with imminent death."

She's in my head. She can read my mind.

"Yes."

The woman's reply was clear, though it possessed a faint echo, originating in the back of Emily's head. It also spoke in Emily's own voice.

Though Emily realized there was no shielding her thoughts from the woman, she felt more comfortable speaking aloud. "Why? Why did this happen?"

After a few moments of silence the woman spoke.

"You are frightened of my countenance. Before I answer, I want you to feel at ease. Briefly, close your eyes."

Emily did as she was told, and when she reopened them seconds later she reared back at the sight. Standing before her was the Virgin Mary.

This visage of the Holy Mother was a duplicate of a picture that hung in Emily's church. She was clothed in an ankle-length white flowing gown, with a matching veil that completely covered her hair. An expansive blue robe, long enough to touch the water, was draped over the woman's shoulders. A strip of blue fabric was cinched across her waist, with the knot tied in front, its two ends hanging free. Her face was beatific, and the bright glow emanating from behind her head left little doubt as to whom the woman wanted Emily to identify her with.

The woman's appearance was sacrilegious, but Emily had to admit it was preferable to the rotting body that she knew actually stood before her. In the recesses of her mind, Emily heard the woman speak.

"I see this is more pleasing."

Emily nodded.

The woman echoed Emily's earlier question. "Why?" A pause, then, "We do it because, like you, we need to feed."

Emily's gut roiled. Visions of hideous creatures feasting on her family immediately came to her, and her face contorted in revulsion. Seconds later the image vanished, and Emily could recall them only vaguely as the woman continued.

"No, that is not who we are. We do not feed on the flesh. We take our nourishment from your life's essence, what you call your soul. It sustains us, allowing us to survive for long periods in the deep. We thrive on your emotions, your moral deliberations, your guilt, and your joy. We relish your ambiguity, delight in your successes, and we question and analyze your failures. We are, in essence, the Christ figure that you have mythologized. We appraise your transgressions, evaluate your responses to them, and we acknowledge your remorse. We grant you absolution. Your souls are the repository of who you are, what you have been. We absorb your souls and you become one with us. It is the only way to insure your eternal, peaceful existence; otherwise, contrary to your beliefs, your souls perish along with your flesh."

Emily trembled, her head shaking violently in denial. The woman's words upended the very tenets of her religion, but as she looked around and viewed the carnage surrounding her, doubt took root in her mind.

If there is a God, would he have allowed this to happen? And, th-these-creatures, surely they could not be God or God-like!

"No." The word was spoken firmly in Emily's head, followed by, "We are not your God."

"Then, who?" Emily asked.

"We are *The Recorders*. Our mission is to gather information. We will be called back one day and asked to share all we have learned, to share all that we have become. When that time occurs, the souls we have taken possession of will not only continue to feed others, but they themselves will be nourished in the sharing."

"The Recorders? Who are you recording for? How long have you been here?"

"We arrived in three sixty-five A.D.—your calendar—in the

region you call Alexandria. After we feed, it takes many years to digest and absorb your souls, so in most cases there are long interludes between harvests. As time progressed so did your science and social skills. We had to adapt or be discovered. Using an empty human vessel, we contact our feeding grounds in advance, make arrangements with them, and offer the majority of their population safety from a harvest as long as we fed on the few. We have found that the threat of annihilation, along with a demonstration of our abilities, always leads to negotiation in our favor."

Emily turned to face the resort below her.

The Virgin Mary nodded. "Yes, they were prepared for us."

Tsunamis. They come in the guise of a tsunami.

Once again, the Virgin Mary nodded. "We do, but not all tsunamis are of our making. Most of them are natural occurrences, harvesting far more souls that we could possibly feed on. With your science so well advanced, you now possess your own recording devices, so we feed in more secluded locations to avoid detection."

"Where do you come from?"

Emily saw what could pass for a smile as the woman replied, "That is not your concern at this moment."

Emily paused, and then asked, "What are you going to do with me?"

The Virgin Mary looked down on Emily, this time with a smile Emily thought to be genuine.

"You are a survivor," the woman began, "and you can remain a survivor if you choose. Shortly, the water will recede and you will be able to continue with your life as it is. However, your husband and children are with us. They, too, will continue to live on. You have a choice to make, but you do not have much time to decide."

With those words, the Virgin Mary began to glide away from Emily. As the woman retreated, her body descended into the depths.

Emily did not react. She continued holding onto the palm tree and watched in silence until the top of the woman's veil disappeared and only calm water remained.

Emily was exhausted. She wanted to rest her forehead against the tree trunk and take some time to think about what had just happened, but as she moved forward she noticed that the water surrounding the trunk was receding. Emily loosened her hold and let the water guide her to the ground.

When Emily's feet touched the beach sand, she relaxed and leaned against the tree for support. She scanned the beach. The water continued to backtrack toward the sea.

"You will have a choice soon, and not a lot of time to make it."

The woman's words echoed through Emily's mind as she watched the ocean ebb. The water made steady progress, and in less than five minutes she thought the beach would be restored to its former size. Emily turned, looking back toward the resort. The staff must have believed the threat over as they were making their way toward her. She saw a mixture of amazement and guilt on their faces, and she wondered how they could all live with themselves after the collective decision they had made. Now, she had a choice of her own to make.

She could pull herself away from the tree and approach the hotel staff, accept their pity, their offers of assistance, and then move on with her life. There would be a price to pay for this, and it would be steep. She would be forever trying to suppress the images of the death and destruction during her waking hours, and unable to banish the terror of it all in her nightmares. The images of Stephen and Carl crushed into the sand and the horror of Samantha taken away could never be shared with anyone back in New Hampshire. No one would believe her.

As she had done so often in her life when she was besieged with doubt, she grasped the cross hanging from her neck. Instead of gaining solace from the icon, Emily felt empty, lost. The gold cross had always been a tangible reminder of her faith, giving her strength or, at the very least, hope in times of trouble or confusion. Now it was just a piece of cheap jewelry weighing heavily against her chest. For a brief moment, anger flared. How could she have been so misled all these years? How could she have been so naïve and trusting?

Emily looked out over the beach. The water had receded quicker than she had thought it would, and the shoreline almost looked as it had before the tsunami.

Gazing up, Emily saw the woman, the true form of the woman, standing on top of the ocean a short distance away. The woman's stance appeared casual, neither beckoning nor reproachful. She was waiting.

A vision appeared in Emily's mind. Though the image fluttered as if it were drifting along casually on an ocean wave, she had no problem identifying it. The three of them—Carl, Stephen, and Samantha—were all standing together on a mountaintop staring off into a night sky glittering with starlight. They appeared to be at peace, and judging from the looks on their faces, in a state of spiritual awe.

Emily made her choice.

She tore the cross from her neck and threw it to the ground.

Gathering her strength, she sprinted to the shoreline. When the water was up to her knees, she dove in, swimming toward the woman. Kicking her legs hard and taking broad strokes to reach her, Emily pushed forward. The thought of reuniting with her family provided enough fuel to keep her tired body from burning out. Her life would not be worth living if she couldn't feel the warmth of her husband's love or experience the joy her children brought her. This was her chance to be reunited with them, and she would not be denied.

When Emily had covered half the distance to the woman, she felt a tug on her left leg. She ignored it at first, but when it happened again she couldn't dismiss it. Whatever had been tugging at her pulled her completely underwater. After flailing for a moment, she rose back up and treaded water. An odd tingling in her left thigh had her hand reaching down to it. She felt nothing wrong so she continued along the length of her leg. When her fingers brushed her ankle she paused, a feeling of dread passing through her. The flesh at her ankle was torn, and it felt stringy. Below the ankle, her foot was gone. Stunned, she probed the area, and when her fingers touched exposed nerves, pain ricocheted throughout her body. The water around her was turning red. There was another tug, a more powerful one this time, and she was dragged deep into the water. She looked down, and saw that her leg, up to her knee, had been torn from her body. Her mouth opened in a scream and seawater rushed in. Her body bucked wildly as she gagged, and the torrents of blood pumping from the stump made the water too hazy to see through.

A voice, sounding like her own, entered her mind. There was no mistaking its mocking tone.

"You are very gullible."

Confusion now kept company with Emily's pain. Why would this woman go through all this trouble to torment her? The woman had plenty of opportunity to kill her earlier, why had she been toyed with?

The answer to Emily's questions came swiftly.

"I enjoy playing with my food."

As she tried to make sense of the woman's words, new images flashed in Emily's mind. They were of the last moments of her life, only in reverse order. She saw herself swimming toward the woman, seeking salvation and hoping to be reunited with her family. Then she was on the beach, watching the resort staff making their way toward her. Next, she was holding on to the palm tree and watching as the dead were dragged down into the water. She watched as Samantha was pulled from her hands. Following that, she saw her husband and son crushed by the giant tubes of water. The next image to fill her mind lingered longer than the others. It was of her floating motionless in the water, a large shard of glass protruding from her head as the water darkened, and Samantha nearby, crying.

When that last image flickered away, Emily realized who the woman really was.

Emily slowly brought her right arm to her chest, then, reaching out with her fingers, she placed them just below her neck. Her fingertips moved tentatively, searching for what she believed would be her true salvation.

Emily's fingers came up empty.

The next words she heard only served to increase her suffering.

"Unlike faith, old habits die hard, don't they, Emily?"

At the time I wrote this, there was a lot on the news about transgender and gay rights. I was thinking about how a homophobic and insecure straight man would feel if he was turned into a woman against his will. I wrote the story and kept it somewhat tame, but I put a noir spin on it to give it a feeling of dread and emotional distance. I sent the story to Paul Fry for his Tales of Obscenity *magazine and he accepted it. Paul later changed the name of the magazine to* Beware The Dark *and the story was published there. Not only was I pleased my name graced the cover, but I was also following a story by the horror legend, Ed Lee.*

When my contributor's copy came, I read Ed Lee's lead story first. Oh-My-God! It was one of the most explicit stories I had ever read, almost as graphic as his infamous story, "The Pig". I wondered what readers would think of my subdued little tale after reading Ed's story.

The few reviews of the magazine I had read mentioned my story, and they did so favorably. I was very proud of those reviews and my inclusion in Beware The Dark, *but to this day I don't dare share a copy of the magazine with my family.*

THE BLACK DRESS

Dash stood red-faced at the end of the bed, his arms rigid and his hands drawn into fists. His entire upper body stiffened in frustration. There they were again, her clothes, lying neatly arranged and flat against the bedspread. Anger began to gather, forming a tight ball within his chest, so he took a deep breath. After exhaling, he tried to focus, to calm himself by ridding his mind of the hate he had for that woman. The memories of her infidelity burned and seeing the clothing only stoked his fury.

The sight of her black mini dress, the cleavage-exposing bra, her thong panties, the dark-as-sin nylons, and her three-inch heels did not excite him. In fact, it had the opposite effect. The very sheerness of the dress, the velvety smoothness of her undergarments, and the liquid sheen reflecting off the deep midnight hue of her shoes only taunted him. They were an unwelcome parting gift, a potent reminder of his lack of masculine qualities and his feeble sexual prowess.

Dash had killed her a little over two months ago.

His wife's constant belittling and snide references had worn him down to where he had thought of nothing but killing her. But until that warm July night those many weeks ago, he hadn't had the guts. It was her innuendo of a lover, a casual and cruel utterance after a particularly intense round of verbal bickering that pushed him over the edge.

That evening, after their argument, he followed her to Garbo's, a nightclub in the city, and waited outside, unseen, until she exited with a man. The two took separate cars to a condo on the east side of town where they spent hours together before she left. When he had saw his wife, her hair askew and a smile on her face, walking back toward her car in those very same three-inch spiked heels that now stood upright on the bedspread, Dash's anger had reached its boiling point. He raced toward her from behind and struck her in the head with a tire iron.

Careful to avoid making it appear to be a crime of passion, he grabbed his wife's purse and fled. After disposing of any evidence that could be tied to him, Dash rushed back to their home.

Much to his amazement and relief, he seemed to have gotten away with it.

The police came to his home early the next morning with the news of his wife's death. After they presented him with the apparent facts of her murder, he pretended to be inconsolable. After a brief interview, they left, believing him to be in an appropriate state of grief.

He had seen the detectives only twice after that—once when he went to the station to identify her and retrieve her clothes, and again prior to her cremation when they told him that they had found DNA evidence on his wife. However, they explained to him that it was unlikely that this person was the individual who had robbed and murdered his wife. They continued with the assumption that it was a purse snatching gone horribly wrong.

Dash demanded to know more about the DNA evidence. The detectives explained that his wife had been with another man on the night of her murder and that they had engaged in sexual intercourse. The man admitted he was with Dash's wife the night of the murder but claimed he had nothing to do with it. A lie detector test confirmed that he had told the truth. They would not reveal the man's name, but Dash recognized him at the funeral. After finding out his wife's lover's name, Dash did a search on him. The man was wealthy, of South American descent, and a collector of artifacts dealing with a cult-like religion called Santeria.

The two months after Dash had killed his wife, all was right in his world. The police had left him alone, he had received the benefits from his wife's insurance policy, and he had basked in the solitude that befits a newly single man.

It all turned to shit five nights earlier.

Walking into his bedroom one evening, he saw her clothes had been placed on the bed. They were clean, pressed, and set out as if in preparation for a night on the town. They were the same clothes he had discarded shortly after retrieving them from the police station. He quickly searched the bedroom, wondering if whoever had done this was still in his apartment. Satisfied he was alone, he stood at the foot of the bed, reached down and touched the dress.

A charge like static leapt from the dress into his fingers. He quickly pulled his hand back, but the shock neither ceased nor dissipated. Instead it traveled throughout his body, igniting nerves. His head had received the brunt of the pain, feeling as if thousands of tiny needles were rolling around in his skull. His eyes watered, and like the shutter on a high speed camera, he blinked rapidly and uncontrollably.

That's when he saw her at the other end of the bedroom, flickering images in black and white, naked and smiling.

His wife had glided toward him, approaching as if she were illuminated by a strobe light. With every flash she neared until her face was directly in front of his. She reached out with her hand and touched his face.

And the pain stopped.

As his heart rate slowed and his vision returned to normal, Dash took a moment to get his bearings. But even when all the after-effects of the incident had left him, he knew something had changed. He felt a bit off; his equilibrium shaky and his thinking cloudy. As he tried to concentrate, to make sense of what was happening to him, his body went rigid. Then, as if a great weight had taken residence in his mind, his head was forcibly bowed—his chin pressed against his chest. A gauntlet of emotions, all foreign to him, exploded into his consciousness.

Initially he was frightened, but soon this passed and gave way to bewilderment. And then, inexplicably, he felt foolish. The assault continued, until finally, he surrendered to the strongest emotion to assail him yet…compulsion.

Dash stripped off his pajamas and, very slowly and sensuously, affixed the bra to his chest. He slipped on the panties and then, sitting on the end of the bed, he slowly slid the nylons up his calf. Smoothing out the hose, he shimmied into the dress. Lastly, his feet gently glided into her high heels.

Glancing in the mirror hanging on the bedroom door, he saw his reflection and was disgusted. His wife's face gazed back at him.

Tonight, as she had done for the past five evenings, she would force Dash out into the night, to the clubs, and into her lover's arms until morning.

I have received more comments on this story than any other I had written. Some readers get it, but many do not. It was meant to be a darkly humorous piece, and written around the time I wrote "The Black Dress". I remember when I presented the story to my writers group all but one chuckled uncomfortably. The one member who had appreciated it, Cat Pragoff, had worked for the American Korean Foundation (an American charity that raised funds for South Korean children) and she corrected some of the clothing names I had used. I had relied on the internet to get the names right and Cat saved me from certain embarrassment.

After I finished the story, I sent it to Christopher Jones for his opinion. I remember his response distinctly. It was a simple, "Wow." I didn't know what it meant, and I didn't ask. When Eulogies II was looking for submissions, I sent him a different story. He replied that he liked it, but did I still have the Korean sex story available? I had submitted "Chiyoung and Dongsun's Song" to someone else but it had been held for ten months without a response. I emailed the publisher and asked if I could have the story back—and they agreed. I let Chris and Nanci Kalanta have the story and it was shortly after when they asked if I would like to join them as an editor for the Eulogies series of anthologies.

CHIYOUNG AND DONGSUN'S SONG

As was the custom in the 16th century, the villagers of Hahoe, Korea, were busy making festival preparations for *Sol-nal*, the ceremonial holiday that ushered in the New Year. The three-day celebration called for much work; the men gathered food for the great feast while the women joined circles to weave decorations for the celebratory dance held on the final day.

But on this late afternoon, as the men harvested the grain and the women worked the straw, Lee Chiyoung and Kim Dongsun were not among them.

Chiyoung was the pretty and precocious daughter of one of the more honored clans in the village, and Dongsun was the hard-working son of a farming family. It was Chiyoung who had suggested a meeting at the clearing in the forest bordering their village, and Dongsun all too willingly agreed.

Dongsun, barely able to contain his excitement, had slipped away from his work group and arrived early.

He leaned back against a large boulder in the middle of the clearing, loosened the *jeogori* that draped his upper body, and waited anxiously for Chiyoung. He had dreamt of her often, spending many an evening on his cot with a hand slipped into his *baji* while fondling himself. Earlier that morning, when she teasingly offered to meet him in the woods, Dongsun believed his fantasies had come true.

Though Dongsun believed he truly loved Chiyoung, he was no fool. It was no secret that Chiyoung delighted in exploiting her desirability, often meeting with the other boys in the village—sometimes the men. For his part, Dongsun understood he was merely one of many apples on a tree waiting to be picked. However, Dongsun had hoped that after this meeting his love for Chiyoung would be requited, that she would forsake her ways and choose him as her life partner.

Dongsun's thoughts turned from her promiscuity to her emerald eyes, her full lips, and her large breasts. His anticipation grew.

While Dongsun waited impatiently for her arrival, Chiyoung stood before a long reflecting glass inspecting her features. As an only child, Chiyoung was fortunate enough to have her own private area and, as the grandchild of a village elder, she was blessed with many gifts. Adornments for her long braided hair and colors for her face were the most common and she put some of these to use knowing with certainty that they would assist with her seduction. Believing she could not improve upon her facial beauty, she focused on her clothing.

She inspected her jeogori. The blouse clung tightly and she was satisfied with the way it highlighted her breasts. She spun around rapidly causing the chima hanging from her waist to swish about, exposing her legs suggestively. She reached back and moved her braid so it hung before her, and then she caressed it with both hands as she gazed at herself in the glass. She smiled approvingly at her reflection. She hoped that Dongsun was worth all the effort. Content with her appearance, she quickly draped on a durumagi to provide some warmth and then stealthily made her way through the village and to the clearing.

Dongsun watched eagerly as Chiyoung emerged from the wooded path. As she strode toward him, his heart leapt, and when she smiled, all else vanished except her face.

"I don't have much time," Chiyoung whispered as she drew him near.

Their arms swiftly encircled one another and they bent their heads forward until their lips touched. Dongsun parted his teeth slightly when he felt her probing tongue.

A rustling of branches somewhere close by drew their attention. They broke apart nervously, surveying the area for onlookers. They saw no one.

Dongsun, eager to continue the embrace, proclaimed it a deer and that there was nothing to fear. With a laugh, Chiyoung responded, "It might be a Dokkaebi. He's a trickster and we'd best be careful."

Dongsun knew the lore of the Dokkaebi, as did every child

who grew up in the village. He had always dismissed it as an old women's folk tale. The Dokkaebi were imps who would grant a wish for a favor given, but the wish was not always granted in the way one hoped for. It was the generosity of the favor and the whim of the Dokkaebi that determined the outcome.

The last thing Dongsun wanted to be thinking about was imaginary imps, so he once again embraced Chiyoung. To his relief, she allowed herself to be held and relaxed in his grip.

Chiyoung surrendered herself, but not because it was Dongsun holding her. It could have been any boy and she would have done the same.

It was soon after her first bleeding that she found herself craving the touch of a boy. She had gone out of her way to initiate physical contact with them, sometimes to the point of making them feel uncomfortable. As time passed, those cravings grew, and a young girl's yearnings for affection were replaced with a woman's desire for more.

Chiyoung broke from Dongsun's embrace and lowered herself until she was on her knees. With practiced fingers she slid her hands to the top seam of his baji and untied its drawstring. Chiyoung folded her fingers around his waist and pulled the baji down around Dongsun's ankles.

All afternoon Dongsun had thought of nothing else but this encounter. Even though he had fantasized that Chiyoung would use her mouth on him, he was unprepared for the amount of sexual tension he was experiencing. He had to concentrate very hard to keep his seed from spilling as Chiyoung lowered his *baji*.

What Dongsun hadn't anticipated, however, was Chiyoung's abrupt halt of all activity after his manhood was exposed. She knelt before him unmoving, without sound.

Confused, he waited.

After a moment, Chiyoung rose from her kneeling position. With a deep frown etched on her face, she made quick eye contact with Dongsun and then looked away.

Dongsun's concern about spilling his seed evaporated.

"I am sorry, Dongsun," Chiyoung explained coldly, "but you are too small. I need something larger to satisfy me. You should try with some of the other girls in the village who have not been with boys yet. They may be suitable for someone of your size."

Abruptly, Chiyoung turned from him and then hurried down the path back to the village.

Dongsun's confusion turned to shock, then disappointment, and finally embarrassment. Still standing against the boulder with his *baji* draped around his ankles, he did the only thing he could think to do. Dongsun cried.

And that's when a Dokkaebi made its appearance.

The imp, dressed lightly for the season and carrying a small club, sprinted from the path and up to Dongsun. "I saw what happened, boy, and I will say that you have made my day a good one as I admit to being amused."

Dongsun wiped his tears away with the back of his hand and gaped at the creature, until finally, curiosity got the best of him. Dongsun asked the creature if the tales he had heard as a child about the Dokkaebi were true.

"They are true young man. I will grant you your wish, but I will need a favor to my liking."

"I want to be the one she desires," Dongsun sobbed.

"And what can you give me in trade?" the imp asked

Dongsun had nothing of value to offer the Dokkaebi, so a feeling of despair gripped him. Then, looking at the creature, he noticed that the imp was poorly dressed for the cold.

"I will give you my *jeogori*," Dongsun offered.

The Dokkaebi frowned. "That is the deal then?"

"Yes, it is all I have to offer."

The last thing Dongsun remembered before the world turned black was the imp rushing at him with his club held high.

Chiyoung woke from an uneasy sleep.

After abandoning the tryst with Dongsun, she had hurried home and lay on her mattress. Then, using the images of a man who had once satisfied her, she administered the relief she had so desperately sought from Dongsun. Finally sated, she napped, but instead of a restful slumber she tossed and turned. Chiyoung's dreams were of Dongsun and the horrible way she had treated him

It was the music from the festivities that woke her. The rhythm of drums and the reedy sounds of wind instruments had invaded her dreams, and slowly, sleep broke its claim on her. As she awoke, Chiyoung felt odd, different somehow. As she tried to determine the nature of the change, she noticed an unusual pressure on her thigh. Believing it to be an insect, she absent mindedly reached down to lift her *chima* and remove the object, but when her fingers brushed it, she gasped. Startled, she jumped up and ran to the reflective glass and tore her *chima* from around her waist. She stared in shock at her reflection.

Hanging between her thighs was a penis. A very long penis and it was attached to her.

On the verge of panic, she moved it slightly to the side. A bulging sack of flesh drooped low behind it. Cupping the sack with her hand, two round objects nestled in her palm.

This couldn't be possible! She removed her hand from the testicles and gripped the penis, angling it up for a better look. She screamed. There was a face on the tip of the penis. It was Dongsun's. She stared at it in horror as it emitted a squeaking sound. The face was talking to her! In a daze, she bent to hear his voice.

"Do you love me now, Chiyoung?" he asked.

Somehow, Chiyoung understood. Tears flowed down her cheeks as she gazed at Dongsun. One of them landed on his face and she used her fingers to wipe him dry. Then she stroked him gently, comforting him.

Dongsun rose toward her.

Chiyoung thought about the life ahead of her and how it would be different. She knew that somehow, this was all her fault—a punishment for her sinful ways. But those thoughts vanished as Dongsun, now fully erect, and smiling, stared at her with eyes that begged for acceptance.

And he felt so good.

Chiyoung grinned, wiped away her remaining tears with one hand, and answered his question. "Yes, Dongsun," she moaned as she stroked him harder, "I think I do love you."

Not too far away, standing by a boulder in the woods, a Dokkaebi, wearing a *jeogori* that was much too large for him, laughed like the devil.

"Husband of Kellie" was the first complete story I ever wrote. I sent it to Shroud Magazine and the editor, Tim Deal, said it was great! He loved the story but thought it was too short and asked if I could make it longer. I panicked and tacked on a terrible ending. He never replied to me. I rewrote "Husband of Kellie", lengthened and stuck a better ending on it, then filed the story away, never to submit the tale again. Five years later, Craig Cook was putting together his Piercing the Darkness anthology and he asked me for a story. I had nothing at the time, but then I remembered "Husband of Kellie" and I sent the story to him. He loved it. The strange thing was when I originally wrote "Husband of Kellie", I had deliberately made his wife the lead character in the story and he was the zombie. We were Horror World pals and it was my way of nodding to him. It's funny how some things come full circle.

HUSBAND OF KELLIE

A solitary figure, that of a frail young woman, stood with her head bent low in the snows of the old New Hampshire graveyard. Her exposed hands were sepia tinted and numb. They trembled from a combination of the biting north winds and the weight of the cold steel resting in her arms. With glassy eyes, she once again read the inscription carved into the headstone before her.

CRAIG COOK
HUSBAND OF KELLIE
1975 – 2010

The woman shuddered. Memories, blunt as rusty ice picks, punched into her thoughts.

Her husband, smiling as he walked out the door, tells her not to worry, that with the new protocols enacted against the epidemic he was guaranteed to come home to her safely.

Then hours later, when embracing him at their front door, she realized his return was due to instinct, and not any promises he had made her.

A motion below her feet pulled her back into the present. She blinked softly and focused on the ground. It was barely perceptible at first, but yes, there it was. The snow was breathing.

She took a cautionary step backward, paused, and even though it was expected, she screamed when the ground in front of her erupted.

Two fists thrust up through the ground like twin volcanoes, creating a scattershot of debris that turned the surrounding snow black.

The young woman stood her ground and watched the resurrection despairingly as a set of arms followed the fists, and moments later, the rest of her husband rose from his grave.

He stood before her, his eyes locked onto hers.

The young woman stared back, seeking recognition, but all she found in his eyes was hunger. She braced herself and weakly raised the shotgun that had been nestled in her frozen hands. As she aimed, her arms trembled, and her thoughts once more flashed back to her husband's explanation of the new protocols.

He spoke casually, telling her that newly discovered drugs managed to delay reanimation of the recently dead for thirty-six hours. Bodies were to be buried in a shallow grave without a coffin. When the drug wore off, someone, even if it was a relative, must be present to terminate reanimation. She saw herself nodding her head in agreement with him when he wondered somberly how a family member could do something so hideous to someone they loved.

The young woman's thoughts were chased away when she heard grunting. She was startled by the realization that he was calling her name.

Her husband shuffled awkwardly toward her with his arms outstretched, his eyes wide, and his mouth opened impossibly wide.

Kellie pulled the trigger.

With tears flowing, she lowered the shotgun and mouthed the words, "I love you, Craig."

Then Kellie turned slowly to face the entrance of the cemetery. Gazing at the gates, she began to speak once more, "And I love you, too, Da…"

A second shot echoed through the graveyard, the bullet penetrating Kellie's heart and exiting through her back. Red streaks accented the black-and-white palette of the gravesite. Kellie's body slipped slowly to the ground as if she were a blanket covering and comforting her husband.

A man, middle-aged and dressed in hunters' orange, lowered his high-powered rifle and leaned it against the cemetery's fence. His shoulders sunk low to the ground and his chest tightened as he struggled to control the sobs that racked his body.

Grabbing the tip of the rifle barrel and then dragging it along behind him, the man walked to his pickup truck parked near the cemetery's entrance. The snow parted in whispers as he forced his boots ahead of him along the covered walkway, the butt of his rifle leaving its own wake. Reaching the truck, he placed the rifle into the rack in the back seat and then picked up a shovel that was stored in the bed.

Walking toward the gravesite he remembered the phone call from his daughter three days ago.

She had told him how Craig had come home early from an errand, bloodied, bitten, and incoherent. She didn't think twice about attending to his wounds and risking infection. When it was apparent that he would soon die, she had kissed her husband one last time before he passed. Only after Craig had drawn his last breath did she call him, and only to ask if he would finish this for her. And then she spoke of her mother, about how much she loved her, and how she didn't think her mother would understand what needed to be done.

As the man approached his daughter's body, only one question now occupied his thoughts. How would he tell his wife what he had done? How, she would ask, could a father ever have done something so terrible to his own daughter?

And then he wondered what his wife would say to him when he told her he would have to do it all over again, only thirty-six hours from now.

This was the first story I had professionally published. Nanci Kalanta, who owned Horror World back then, read the story and thought it creepy enough to publish. I owe Nanci an awful lot, and publishing "An Alabama Christmas" is the least of my debt.

AN ALABAMA CHRISTMAS

It was time for Margaret Cole to watch the death of another day.

Groaning from the ache of fatigued muscles, Margaret rose from an old oak chair. After tucking it under the table, she ambled over to her kitchen window hoping that the short walk would iron out some of the kinks in her legs. Instead, when her belly touched the kitchen's counter, her legs continued complaining. Sighing, she placed her hands on the windowsill for balance and then edged forward until her elbows rested on the yellowed counter. Letting go of the windowsill, she made fists and peered out the window.

Margaret allowed herself a few moments to gaze at the majesty of the skyline. The remnants of sunset had colored the distant clouds with a reddish-brown hue; it was a stunning contrast to the ever-deepening blanket of night. As impressive as the sight was, she had more important reasons to peer out the window. Cocking an ear, she realized that the birds had already ceased their singing, their melodies replaced by the sounds of the evening. She listened intently to the chirping of crickets and the mating calls of the peepers. Margaret had seen a multitude of Alabama suns die in her lifetime and she wondered as she lent her ear to this evening's serenade, was she watching her last? Would he come for her again tonight?

Since her childhood, he had always come to her on this night. Though she knew he aged, in her mind his countenance hadn't changed since that first night when he arrived with a smile and the promise of delivering the best gift she could ever have imagined. But from the moment she laid eyes on him, dressed cheerfully in a bright red suit and a stocking cap balanced crookedly on his head, she hadn't been fooled. When he had motioned with his free hand to the pillowcase slung casually over his shoulder, telling her it was stuffed with boxes wrapped in gold foil and topped with ribbons made from tinsel, she hadn't been tempted with his gifts. Margaret vividly remembered her young self backing away from him, recoiling in terror to the farthest corner of the room. It was her earliest memory, one that was cursed to be replayed yearly over the next fifty years of her life.

As Margaret peered out her window, her elbows slipped and her head dropped. It occurred to her that the weight of her thoughts might have been too much for her arms to support. Her eyelids drooped heavily. In a moment of fatigue, she was tempted to say a prayer.

Margaret snapped her head up quickly, forced her eyes to open wide, and she inhaled deeply. Prayers had never prevented his arrival before and she doubted whether they would work now. Silently, she vowed, *things were going to be different this year.* If he did come back, she was going to fight him this time, not give in as she had in the past. Her preparations had begun months ago, and though she believed everything she had done up to now would prevent another visit, she could not take any chances. There was more to do. She returned her attention outdoors and watched the darkness claim the night. It soothed her and, feeling calmer, she began to review her plans.

Margaret took comfort that the old ways would more than suffice in granting her security this evening. In this modern world of intruder alarms and electronic eyes, she would rely on nature. Gazing at the leafy maples and the densely shaded elms, she noted the absence of even a gentle breeze. She thought that this would aid in her defense. For that she was grateful, despite the simmering heat and the perspiration dotting her brow.

Her farmhouse, a large and sturdy ranch built by her father shortly before he married her mother, was situated in a valley surrounded by nests of scrub and a forest full of hardwood. The trees were packed so densely that even the slightest wind could set them to conspire. Their whispering would have caused enough of a din to make it difficult to listen for him. She needed the trees to be still so she could better hear the sounds of encroachment. She would be listening for a snap of a twig, the swish of a boot parting leaves, or the scuttle of pebbles. Any of these things would cause her alarms to go off. All she had to do was listen and take note of any sudden silence from the insects and the peepers.

Margaret reached up and pulled the thin, sun-bleached, rose-colored drapes of the kitchen window further apart, leaving as wide a view as possible, then she returned to her seat in the living room. Earlier, she had done the same to all of the windows in the house, exposing the interior of her home with the understanding that their flimsy panes of glass were not going to prevent his visit. She had also left the front and rear doors propped open. Margaret knew the open doors and windows could be construed as an invitation, but she had no choice. She needed to hear the approach of her visitor if he came before she was ready. It could give her precious moments to prepare for the confrontation. Despite everything she had done earlier to prevent his arrival, she wanted to leave nothing to chance.

Sitting at the table, Margaret concentrated on an old book before her, one that her grandmother had written weeks before she had died of consumption. Her grandmother was the only person she had ever confided about the visitor. She did so reluctantly, and only after her grandmother had noticed Margaret's sudden withdrawal from any conversation having to do with this night. Her grandmother had been shocked when she heard Margaret's story and voiced her concern. But she confessed to Margaret that the visitor was a tradition in her family, and as Margaret grew older and wiser, the visits would cease.

Margaret was stunned last October when, while searching for a shovel in the woodshed, she discovered the hand-bound book bearing her name at the bottom of an old trunk. The book she reasoned, along with an urn holding her grandmother's ashes, a few pamphlets containing recipes, and an assortment of other meager possessions, might have been left in the trunk for Margaret to open when she was older. She thought the trunk must have been tucked away in the corner of the outbuilding after the old woman died and then forgotten. Storage in the shed had subjected the book to one hell of a beating though, and Margaret was ever so thankful that it hadn't been destroyed outright.

The book's cover was as yellowed as her mother's bridal gown that still hung from a wooden peg in her parents' bedroom. Because its pages were as brittle as the dried flowers adorning her front door, she took great care when fingering and turning the pages. She had to squint to make out the words as the ink used for the script had faded so much. The book itself was only ten pages, but she reread only the portion she hoped would protect her, if warranted, on this night. Though the text she needed to memorize was only two pages long, any deviation from those written words could produce results that were unexpected, not to mention extremely dangerous to her.

After spending hours rereading the pertinent passages of the book, she thought herself ready. She closed her eyes, bowed her head, and moved her lips in time with her thoughts as she tested her memory. After repeating the complete text several times without error, she felt confidence building within her.

But the sensation was fleeting; something caused a chill to travel up her spine.

She cocked her head and concentrated. It took only a few seconds to understand what had happened. The sounds of the night were gone. The crickets had ceased their leg beatings and the frogs had gone silent.

Her alarms were triggered.

She was out of time.

Margaret's eyes opened and she lifted her head, turning toward the front door. As she stared at it, the silence rested heavily on her shoulders. Then, there it was—a snap. A branch was broken underfoot, somewhere above her. She glanced to the roof and scanned the crossbeams and pine planking. She held her breath. There was a footstep, and then another. In their wake, small clouds of dust floated to the floor.

He was coming.

She rose from the chair and took baby steps toward the front door, making as little noise as possible. She couldn't alert him to her presence just yet. Every second counted. Pausing a few feet from the door, Margaret prepared herself for the incantation. She assumed a position of strength, jutting her chest forward and pulling in the small of her back. Her spine stiffened and she closed her eyes.

Instantly, Margaret became aware of her bulk. Her knees shook from the strain of her weight and her feet cramped. As uncomfortable as the position was, it gave her a feeling of being grounded, of having roots that would steel her for what was to come.

She lifted her arms straight out from her sides, her head rising in conjunction with them. When her limbs were even with her shoulders, she opened her palms and spread her fingers wide. She spoke, murmuring the incantation that she had spent the last few months committing to memory. Standing as still as a statue of Christ, she focused all of her energy on the recitation.

Though she tried to shut out all else while she concentrated on the words that flowed through her lips, she could still hear her visitor's footsteps on the roof. The dust, which she felt falling onto her, continued to rain in pockets from the ceiling. His footfalls were almost directly overhead.

Margaret reached the end of the incantation, but then repeated it, speaking faster and louder. Nearing completion of the second recitation, she raised her arms higher, until they were parallel with her body. She clasped her hands together and folded her fingers into each other. After the last sentence, she paused for a breath, opened her eyes, and spoke one more word in a beseeching tone that had not been part of the incantation.

"Please," she whispered.

The sound of the footsteps ceased.

Margaret lowered her head and dropped her arms. She remained cautious and tense. She stood motionless, stared ahead, focused on the area outside of her front door. Minutes passed without any sign of her visitor. She relaxed her shoulders and allowed her body to sag. When she heard the sounds of crickets and peepers returning to their nightly chorus, tears of relief trickled down her cheeks.

The returning sounds of the night were soon joined by another.

Margaret's screams drowned out the insects' cacophony. Four fingers, clothed in a red glove, snaked in from outside the door and clutched at its wooden frame.

"Noooooooo...!" Margaret moaned as she squeezed her eyes shut and dropped to her knees in defeat. Her body shook from the hammering of her heart and the churning in her belly. She clutched her stomach to prevent its contents from spilling. With both arms draped around her midriff, she rocked her upper body like a child trying to deal with reality. Amidst the pain and the confusion, Margaret was slipping into darkness.

It was the bitter taste of salt from her tears that brought her around. Though her body shuddered and her mind struggled with fear, Margaret forced herself to open her eyes. A lifetime of torment should have ended this night—she did everything she was supposed to do. She had spoken the incantation to the letter; she had made no mistakes. Why did he come back? She needed to see the rest of him, to see if anything she had done had worked. She lifted her head and faced the doorway.

Using the door's frame for leverage, her visitor pulled his body into view. He now stood fully in the doorway. Using the last vestige of her strength, Margaret screamed once again.

In the past, the overly large coat and trousers her visitor wore had held his ample girth. Their color, a glossy bright red had complimented the pair of black spit-polished boots he had worn. She recalled that his long curly hair, downy beard, and wide belt were always as white as freshly fallen snow, easily matching the brilliance of the puff ball on top of his stocking cap and the pillowcase slung over his shoulder. This night, it was different.

His suit was draped loosely over his gaunt frame. The coat was many sizes too large. Around his legs she saw his trousers hung loosely, cinched tightly with twine to prevent them from falling. His coat and pants were still a deep shade of red but their luster was gone, dull as the faded curtains in her kitchen. The pillowcase that hung limp and empty off his right shoulder was badly stained, blemished by something that resembled the color of urine. But it wasn't his attire that made Margaret scream—it was his face.

Strings of decayed flesh hung from his cheeks, clotted with clumps of dried blood and dark soil. Small fissures pockmarked his forehead and neck, some filled with that same, earthy soil, others teaming with worms. When she met his eyes, she saw they were yellow. Maggots gave the illusion they were in constant motion.

Her visitor appreciated her studied gaze. He formed a smile through grated lips. When he lowered his jaw to speak, a mouthful of maggots tumbled out and fell to the floor.

"Hello Margaret."

"No—no—no!" On her knees, Margaret sobbed. She weakly pointed a finger at her visitor, her chest convulsed and her voice stammered as she spoke. "I did everything the book asked me to do. Grandmother put it all down for me. I read the words. I read the words.... I started months ago. I—I—killed you—Daddy—I killed you!"

"....Margaret..."

"I plunged a knife into you while you slept. I stuck it into you over and over again. I—I cut your heart.... I cut out your heart out." Margaret's face went rigid with anger and she jabbed her finger at him and shrieked, "I CUT YOUR HEART OUT, DADDY!"

Margaret slumped, and rested her rump on her heels. Her hands fell to her side. She spoke in a daze.

"Your blood—it—it was everywhere. But I didn't stop—no, I didn't stop. I mashed it into a pulp." She brought both her hands above her head, clasped them together, and once again found herself pleading as loud as her voice would allow. "DON'T YOU UNDERSTAND, DADDY? I MASHED YOUR HEART INTO A PULP. I USED A HAMMER AND I MASHED YOUR HEART INTO A PULP!"

Margaret's body stiffened then heaved. She threw herself onto the floor and buried her face with her hands. *How could it have all gone so wrong?* But even as she lie there, her body racked with sobs, there was an overwhelming need to find out why the incantation didn't work. She forced herself to speak to him again, her voice lower, just above a whisper. "I—I mixed your heart up with Grandmother's ashes, she told me to do it. It's in the book. She—she thought she could hold you back from returning. I buried the ashes in the field along with the rest of your body along with that—that..." Margaret giggled, "that stupid suit you kept hidden in that pillowcase in the woodshed." She lifted her head from the floor and met his gaze. "Why didn't it work, Daddy? I did everything the book told me to do. I did everything Grandmother asked me to do. She was going to protect me. Why didn't it work?"

With his boots planted firmly in place, her visitor bent forward with a leer. He cocked his head, and then moved it from side to side, studying her through custard eyes. After a moment, he replied, more maggots spilling from his mouth.

"Christmas comes every year Margaret." And then he added, "Everybody knows, you can't stop Christmas from coming."

With a gravelly laugh, her daddy straightened up and Margaret could see an erection jutting through his pants. With a shudder, Margaret's thoughts turned to the worms. As he closed the distance between them, insects trailed him on the floor. He loomed over her, peered down on her prone form, and held a gloved hand out to her. There was no mistaking the tone of parental authority when he said to her, "Let's go into my bedroom, dear. We can celebrate the holiday the same way we have since your mother died when you were a child."

Margaret bowed her head in resignation. She lifted a timid hand to his. His grip was soft and spongy.

"That's a good girl. I've got the same gift for you that I've given you every year, my dear. And I know what you want to give me! It's the same one I always ask of you." As an afterthought, he added, "Let's make it special this year, dear. Is your mother's wedding dress still on the peg?"

And as she had done for the past fifty years, Margaret let her daddy take her hand and lead her into his bedroom. As she walked with him, her thoughts raced back to earlier in the day when she stood at her kitchen sink and gazed at the splendor of the setting sun. No matter how this night might end, Margaret understood that she had indeed watched the death of her last Alabama day.

If you aren't familiar with the author Rex Miller, his signature character is a giant of a man called Chaingang who essentially takes what he wants when he wants it. The image of some hulking brute who could kill anyone with his bare hands stuck with me, and I have always wanted to use a character like him in a story.

One morning, on the way to work, a scene of a man standing in the pouring rain came to me. I invented his backstory during my commute and by the time I got to work, I had figured out how to combine this man's tale of woe with the giant. I sent this story to Wicked Tales, and the editors Scott Goudsward, David Price, and Dan Keohane immediately accepted it.

I don't usually think of sequels or follow-ups to my stories, but I can see myself returning to "The Pawnshop" in the future.

THE PAWNSHOP

Buck stood under a sagging, weather-beaten florist canopy, taking refuge from the rain. A damp and numbing chill had seeped into his spine. Shivering, he absently stroked the outline of his nose. There was no doubt it was broken. He was grateful for the modicum of pain relief from the Advil he had swallowed earlier.

The rain continued to beat hard onto the pavement; it sounded like a million men marching in place as it echoed off the walls. The roar, droning and exceptionally loud, fed a pounding headache. His view was limited to three or four feet as he looked out from the canopy; beyond that, nothing but a shimmering, translucent curtain of falling needles. It didn't prevent Buck from locking his eyes on the pawnshop across the street.

"Do it, or we're going to kill your wife and daughter."

The phrase had played a constant loop in his head for the last hour.

He had left work ten minutes early to hit up the ATM for some extra cash. Tomorrow was his wife's birthday and he wanted to treat her to something special. He withdrew a hundred dollars, enough for them to have a nice dinner, see a movie, and pay the babysitter. It was a lot of money, but he'd been putting a little bit aside for months. Since he walked to and from his job, he used an ATM inside a grocery store, close to where he worked. After stuffing his wallet into his pants pocket, he adjusted the hood on his raincoat and then switched to autopilot for the walk home. His head bowed, he took scant notice of his surroundings.

They came out of nowhere, lying in wait in an alley between two storage buildings. He hadn't felt the blow to his head until after he had kissed the pavement. He remembered trying to utter, "What?" but he never got the chance to pronounce the "t". His eyes had widened and lost focus as they rolled skyward. The muscles in his upper body eased and he slumped forward. There was pressure around his ankles. Then his feet were pulled out from under him. There was no way he could have cushioned the fall and he landed face first onto the sidewalk. He recalled his nose cracking loudly with the impact.

Then the pain hit.

His first reaction had been to gag, but the throbbing in his head overrode the impulse. He clenched his jaw and squeezed his eyes shut trying to will some control over the hammering in his head. As he attempted to isolate and subdue the pain, a fresh source of anguish competed for his attention. His nose erupted in agony as he was dragged along the pavement.

Two sets of hands grabbed his armpits, lifting him off the ground and then shoving him against the side of a building in the alley. As he slid down the wall, his raincoat caught on the bricks, bunching up around his neck and slowing his descent. Someone grabbed the front of his coat, pulled him off the wall, and then assisted him into a sitting position on the ground. The seat of his pants absorbed the rainwater like a sponge, his ass puckered from the sudden chill.

"Shit, man, you hit him too hard."

"No, I didn't. He's just a pussy."

Buck raised his head toward the voices. Groggy, and with rain coming down in torrents, he had a difficult time making out their faces. He blinked rapidly, trying to clear his vision while lifting a hand to the back of his head. The agony was immediate but he continued to probe, assessing the damage. There was a lump, but no broken skin that he could tell.

"Buck, come on, man, snap out of it. I didn't hit you that hard!"

At the mention of his name, Buck turned to the speaker. He didn't recognize the voice. It was low, without any obvious accent. He thought something odd about the man's appearance though, so he focused on his face. After staring for a few seconds, he realized that the man was wearing a mask. It was like the one in that *Halloween* movie, and he tried to think of the character's name. It was Myers, Michael Myers. He turned his head to his left and saw that the other man wore an identical mask.

"Hey, asshole, get it together."

This man's voice was high-pitched, his words spoken fast, almost running into each other. Portuguese, maybe? He worked with some Portuguese, but he couldn't place this guy's voice either.

How do they know my name?

A fist appeared in front of his face.

"Take these." Low-Voice was talking to him. The man opened his hand and Buck saw two brown pills clutched between his fingers. Buck shook his head no.

"It's a pain killer, Advil. Now swallow these, we need you to think clearly."

Buck lifted his free hand and placed it beneath the man's fist. He felt the pills drop into his palm. He stared at them. They looked like Advil. He popped them into his mouth, swallowed, and closed his eyes. When he reopened them, one of the men was on his knees, inches from his face.

"Here's the deal, Buck. We need you to walk on over to the pawnshop on Church Street and get a package for us." It was Low-Voice talking to him again. "He's not going to want to give you the package, so you are going to have to force him to. If he still refuses, you're going to have to get it yourself."

Buck wasn't sure he had heard right. A pawnshop? Get a package? Force him to? Confused, he squinted and cocked his head to the side.

High-Voice jumped into the conversation. "Just do what he says, or you're never going to see your wife and daughter again."

The words got Buck's attention. His eyes swept frantically, back and forth between the two men.

Nanda and Janet? What does this have to do with them?

"We need you to go into the pawnshop and tell the owner you want to buy the Prexy box." It was Low-Voice, picking up where his partner left off. "He will refuse to give it you. If, or I should say when, he does, you get as close to him as you can and threaten him with this." A handgun materialized in front of Buck's face. "There is only one bullet in it and it's meant for the owner of the pawnshop. If you try and use it on one of us, the other one will not only kill you here and now, but then will make a call and have your wife and daughter killed, too. It won't be a quick and easy death for either of them."

Buck could only stare at the duo. How the hell did he get caught up in this nightmare?

Rain ran down Low-Voice's mask as he went on. "We've been watching you for days. And if you're wondering why, it's because you were a convenient choice; it's as simple as that. Now, let's get you up."

Buck was once again lifted by his armpits, his back pushed against the brick wall. His knees were weak, but he managed to stay upright on his own. "Why do you need me?" he asked. "Why can't you guys do it yourselves?"

"He knows us. He's got cameras and would see us coming, even in this rain. It needs to be someone he doesn't know or someone local who he doesn't suspect. You, my friend, fit the bill." Low-Voice said and slipped the handgun into Buck's front pants pocket.

"The safety's off, so be careful. You've only got one bullet and you need to make it count. When he refuses to sell or give you the box, you'll have to kill him and then look for it yourself. A headshot should do the trick. The information we have is that the Prexy box is stored on the top shelf on the wall behind the front counter, but we are not sure of that. The box is made of metal, polished to a shine, so you'll have no problem identifying it when you find it. And don't bother trying to open it. You won't be able to."

Buck looked at Low-Voice and asked, "Do I have to kill him?"

"No. Don't kill him if he sells or gives you the box, but the chances of that are slim. Once you have it, bring it home. We'll be waiting for you there."

"What happens if I can't find the box?"

Low-Voice shook his head.

Buck pleaded with them to spare the lives of his wife and daughter but the two men turned their backs and walked away, heading in the direction of his house. Before turning the corner of the alley, High-Voice turned back to him and shouted, "Do it, or we're going to kill your wife and daughter."

Do it, or we're going to kill your wife and daughter.

So here he was, standing under a canopy, soaked to the gills, building the nerve to cross the street to the pawnshop. The firearm weighed heavily in his pocket. Buck had never fired a gun in his life.

Unanswered questions peppered his thoughts. *What if the pawnbroker wants to sell me the box? How much would he ask for it?* Buck only had a hundred dollars on him. *What happens if the pawnbroker pulls a gun on me?* Maybe he should enter the shop with the gun drawn. *What if I only wound the pawnbroker and then grab the box?* The police would surely understand why, if it came to that. *Who am I kidding? I'm more likely to shoot my own ass off than to hit him!*

Buck surveyed the area in front of the canopy one last time. The view was the same; he couldn't see for more than a few feet in any direction. He thought about fleeing, rushing home, or getting help, but he knew it was not an option. He assumed they were watching him, maybe by someone in one of the cars parked close to the pawnshop or in one of the surrounding buildings. He couldn't take the chance. He was also sure they expected him back at the house in a reasonable amount of time, and he had already burned an hour since they let him go. He had to do this, and he had to do it now; the lives of Nanda and Janet were at stake. Buck adjusted the hood of his raincoat, slipped his hands into his coat pockets, and then he hunched his shoulders.

He winced as he stepped out from under the canopy and into the downpour.

He made his way past the cars parked at the curb, hoping that nobody was foolish enough to be driving in this monsoon. Unable to see much, and with the rain so loud he couldn't hear beyond its roar, he would be a sitting duck. Water rushed down the street in swift currents, high enough that he could feel its wake brush above his ankles, and deep enough to soak a car's brakes to prevent it from stopping.

When he finally reached the sidewalk, his shoulders sagged and he exhaled with relief. He paused to get his bearings, and then he looked up. He was directly in front of the pawnshop, which had a small canopy similar to the florist's. The words GOFFSTOWN PAWN in dark block letters were spread across the front flap. Despite the heavy rain, he could see that the words were as faded as the ones on the florist's canopy. He took a deep breath and walked the few remaining steps to the pawnshop.

Standing beneath the canopy, Buck searched for the cameras. They hung above the entrance door, nestled in its upper corners.

A bright red light glowed in the center of their lenses. An obvious attempt at deterrence, but Buck was dubious of their effectiveness. The owner would only have seconds to react if he spied something suspicious on his video screen, and that's assuming the owner was looking at the screen in the first place.

He stared at the cameras, wondering if he should have walked right into the pawnshop instead of stopping. *Am I being watched now? Is the owner reaching under the counter for a weapon at this moment?* Buck clutched at the gun in his pocket as he pulled the handle of the door.

The interior wasn't what he had expected. Having never been in a pawnshop before, his imagination called up the dirty claustrophobic aisles filled with junk that he had seen in movies and on television. This shop was clean, and the center of the room was so spacious it could have been used as a dance floor. Stainless steel racks with varnished wooden shelves lined the walls, and from what he could see, they contained none of the used tools or old electronic equipment he had envisioned.

Instead, pieces of what he would call art filled the shelves, though not the kind he ever saw hanging on someone's wall or placed on an end table. Brightly colored paintings, appearing Oriental or Egyptian in origin, stood on the shelves in ornate frames. Odd-shaped vases and various small sculptures were also featured prominently on the racks. Buck stood there, his mouth open in wonder, as he gazed at the beautiful but baffling offerings for sale.

"'Lo there, young fellow. How ya doing? You just gonna stand there? How about moving around a bit; you're leaving a puddle on my floor. So, what brings you to my shop on this horrible rainy day?"

The voice was cheery, a bit playful even, and spoken with a slight New Hampshire accent. Buck turned his head toward its source.

A middle-aged man, thin but looking fit, stood behind a counter off to Buck's left. The smile on the man's face complimented his cheery disposition. The counter was long and wide, but Buck noticed it was completely free of merchandise. It began at the window at the front of the store and ran parallel to the wall for ten feet. Behind the counter, more racks with wooden shelves lined the wall. Buck couldn't help himself; he peered along the top shelves, his eyes darting, looking for a polished steel box.

The pawnshop owner's faced dropped. He exhaled and said, "I see." His voice was just above a whisper.

Buck made his way to the counter. He leaned over and placed both his hands flat on top of it. Staring at the man, he said with a slight tremor in his voice, "I need to buy the Prexy box."

"It ain't for sale."

Buck closed his eyes, his face tightening. When he opened them, he begged, "You don't understand—I'm in trouble, real trouble. I need that box!"

The man concentrated on Buck's eyes. "Look, I'm only gonna tell ya this one last time. It ain't for sale. Now, please, leave my establishment." The man's tone was even, but there was no mistaking his insistence.

Buck had dreaded this moment. Frustrated and scared, he felt his body temperature begin to rise. Sweat mingled and beaded with the rain on his forehead. He had no choice. He removed his right hand from the counter and slipped it into his coat pocket. With the grip of the weapon securely in his palm, he pulled it out. He straightened his arm and pointed the gun at the man behind the counter. "I need that box," Buck pleaded. "They are going to kill my wife and daughter if you don't give it to me!"

The hardness behind the man's eyes faded, but Buck thought he could see a gleam in the softening. It was as if the man suddenly found the whole episode amusing. Buck felt uneasy; he began to sway, shifting his weight from leg to leg. There was something odd about this man. He didn't appear fazed by the gun, nor was he moved by Buck's plea. Could it be possible that the man was enjoying this?

"Your wife and daughter…." The corners of the man's lips curled as he repeated Buck's words. "Well, that's a new one." He cocked his head and stared at Buck's face for a few seconds before gazing down at the gun. He paused for a moment longer before continuing. "Okay, I'll do it, but please take a step or two back and lower the weapon. I don't like that thing pointed at me. You're too close; it's making me nervous."

Buck silently thanked God as relief washed over him. He had read the man wrong; the pawnshop owner did care about his wife and daughter. With a weak smile, Buck nodded to the man, lowered his gun hand, and then took two steps back.

Satisfied, the man returned the nod. He reached up with his left hand and moved it sideways, about two feet along the top of the counter. He paused, made a fist, and then stuck out his forefinger. A grin appeared on the man's face as his finger hovered. Confused, Buck tensed. As he watched the man's grin, realization dawned on Buck. Something bad was about to happen. He had no time to question the man, no time to react. The man's finger descended, disappearing into a hole in the counter.

Buck raised his weapon. Before he had the gun level to the man's torso, he heard a rumble above him. The walls of the building began to tremble and he could feel vibrations beneath his feet. A series of crashes, some nearby, others distant, detonated around him. The noise was overwhelming, every crash feeding more pain into his already throbbing head. Buck's hands shot up to cover his ears; the gun's handle pressed tightly against his cheek.

Panicked, he crouched low, his body jerking at the sound of every crash. He caught sight of slight, almost invisible movements, but he couldn't focus on them long enough to see what they were. From the corners of his eyes, he picked up pockets of distortion, as if the air was shimmering, but he saw nothing that would have caused the effect. He lowered his hands from his ears and held onto the gun firmly. He brought the weapon up with both hands, swinging it in wild arcs in the direction of every new crash. His eyes darted back and forth, roaming the shop, looking for anything that might be coming for him.

The chaos ended as quickly as it had begun.

The crashing noises ended without so much as an echo to confirm they had existed. The pawnshop was silent; the only sound Buck heard was a fading ringing in his ears. The building had stopped shaking, and the floor ceased vibrating. He was surprised the air was absent of any dust and the area free of fallen debris. Buck blinked his eyes, swallowed hard, and then took a deep breath. He was alive. Nothing had come for him. He stood from his crouch, gun extended, concentrating on his surroundings. When he finally got a good look at the pawnshop, he was baffled, but he understood what had just happened. He had been played. Lowering his gun, he turned back toward the man at the counter.

A barrier, four feet wide, several inches thick and translucent as glass now stood between Buck and the owner of the pawnshop. Buck's eyes followed the barrier up and saw that it extended through the ceiling. Whatever gears or pulleys were used to lower it must have been on the upper floors, hidden from view. Lowering his head, he saw the bottom of the barrier rested on the floor, the gap so tight a piece of paper couldn't have slipped through. Identical barriers, abutting each other, had descended around the perimeter of the pawnshop. Even if they were manufactured from plastic, they had to be heavy as hell. He could easily see through the barriers, but he did notice faint striations though them. Those imperfections must have caused the movements he caught from the corners of his eyes as the barriers fell.

Buck swiveled his neck from left to right, viewing both ends of the counter. Barriers ran the length of it and they capped off both of its ends. The pawnshop owner was sealed in. The single bullet in his gun was useless.

Buck turned from the man, noticing barriers across the front door, the front window, and in front of every rack. He was caged in. Walking to one of the barriers, he placed his hand on it. As expected, it was solid. Buck had no doubt that it was as heavy as he had imagined. Moving to the middle of the shop, he turned his head in every direction, desperately looking for a way out.

Then he saw one.

There was a break between the barriers, near a corner at the far end of the building. The racks lining the wall had stopped at the break, revealing a recess that was as wide as a barrier. Buck wondered if one of them had failed to drop. He rushed to the opening to check it out, but stopped several feet short. There was always the possibility it could have been a trap. A quick study revealed a dull, metal-plated panel recessed into the wall. He thought it might have been a large door, though he could see no knob or handle.

Deciding that it could be an exit, he took the remaining few steps to the panel. Placing his hands on it, he pushed. It was not going anywhere. As he weighed his options, a noise, sounding like static, screeched from behind him. Buck jumped in place, almost dropping his gun.

"Young fellow, I recommend you back away from there."

It was the pawnshop owner's voice, coming from a tinny-sounding loudspeaker. Turning his head, Buck faced him.

"Please remove yourself to the center of the floor; otherwise I cannot guarantee your survival."

Did he say my survival?

Buck was at a loss. He was in a bad situation and knew it could only get worse. Images of Nanda and Janet flashed in his head. He had never felt as helpless as he did now. With little choice, he obeyed the man and, while keeping his eyes on the door, he walked backward to the center of the floor. When he stopped walking, he heard a buzzing. The door began to move.

Without a whoosh or whisper, the door slipped sideways into the wall. A bright light from behind, irregular in shape, illuminated the edges of the doorway. Standing there, taking up almost the entire space of the opening, was a man, silhouetted from the neck down.

The loudspeaker crackled. "Rex, subdue but don't kill. I want to talk to him."

The figure in the doorway bent down, slowly revealing his head until it was below the top of the doorframe. A man stepped through the opening, then stood up straight. Buck's eyes widened at the sight. Standing before him was a freak of nature. He had to be the biggest man Buck had ever seen in his life. The man was a giant, at least eight feet tall and had to have weighed well over six hundred pounds.

He wore a plain black T-shirt, dark gray sweat pants, and polished black leather boots. The giant's upper body was broad, his shoulders square, but his arms were so muscular that they reminded Buck of The Hulk. The man's hips were as broad as his torso, his legs as thick as tree trunks. The giant was bald with prominently large ears that stuck out perpendicular to his head. His eyes were set wide but they were narrow, and his nose was surprisingly thin. The giant's lips were obese, covering the area from the bottom of his nose to the cleft of his chin. They were pink, fleshy, and dribbled drool.

The giant charged Buck at a speed he didn't think possible for a man that size. Buck's pants got a little wetter. His heartbeat increased, and all thoughts of the pain in his head and nose evaporated. He froze in place, too scared to even think he was going to die. A moment later the giant had one of his massive hands around Buck's throat, lifting him off the floor as if he were weightless. Buck's legs kicked at his attacker, but the blows had as much effect as striking a cement wall. The pressure against Buck's neck increased; he couldn't breathe. His body bucked in its attempt to take in air, and black spots floated in and out of his vision.

The loudspeaker cackled. "Rex! I said I wanted to talk to him!"

The giant turned toward the pawnshop owner. It was difficult to tell from his facial expression, but Buck thought that the giant was not too pleased with the comment. The big man loosened his hold on Buck's throat. The giant then pulled his massive arm back and slightly behind his head. There was a forward motion, and Buck was sailing through the air. He gasped for breath as he braced himself for the impact. When he hit the barrier, Buck saw black as he crumbled to the floor.

When Buck woke, there wasn't a part of him that didn't hurt. His brain felt like a box of rocks and his vision was blurry. As his fog lifted and his eyes focused, he saw the pawnshop owner and the giant bent over, looking down on him. The smaller man had Buck's gun in his hand. "Now," said the pawnshop owner, "what's all this about your wife and daughter?"

Tears rolled out from Buck's eyes. Though his head was cloudy and he had difficulty pronouncing some of the words, he told the man his story. When he finished, the pawnshop owner and the giant straightened up, looked at each other for several seconds, and Buck noticed an unspoken signal passing between them. After the pawnshop owner nodded to the giant, they both helped Buck to his feet. The smaller man addressed Buck.

"If you hadn't guessed by now, they've tried and failed to get the box before. Using you, while a desperate act and not very clever, is, however, somewhat amusing. I assume they do not think your chances very high. This, unfortunately, does not portend well for your wife and daughter. Please, what is the address of your home?"

The pawnbroker's speech caught Buck off guard. The man had lost his New Hampshire accent, and he appeared to be much more sophisticated than Buck had originally thought. With his head starting to swim again, it took Buck a few extra moments to remember his address. Finally Buck gave him the number of his house on Third Avenue.

"Rex and I are going to pay your assailants a visit. You must remain here. I will be turning the lights off and the security system on. I warn you, if you try to leave, you will die. Do not move from where you are, do not touch any of the items on the racks, and do not look for the Prexy box."

Buck gazed around the shop, the fog in his head making it hard to concentrate. He noticed that the barriers were gone. *If they weren't the security system, then what the hell else did this guy have hidden away?* After Buck nodded his response to the pawnbroker, he passed out.

A loud *thunk* revived Buck. Still dazed, he struggled to get his bearings. He took stock of his position, discovering that his back was against a hard surface and that he could see his feet stretched out before him. It took a moment but he realized he had been propped up on the counter in the pawnshop with his back leaning against the front window. Lifting his head, he saw the pawnshop owner, his hair wet and matted, and the giant, his T-shirt drenched, standing on either side of the counter. Buck recalled the pawnshop owner telling him that they were going to his home to pay Low-Voice and High-Voice a visit. Buck wondered how long they were gone.

On the counter, between the pawnshop owner and the giant, rested a polished metal box. It was about one foot square. The pawnshop owner turned toward Buck and grinned when he saw that Buck had come to. The owner then turned back to the giant and nodded.

The giant reached deep into the pockets of his sweatpants. His hands fumbled until he pulled from each pocket something that Buck could only describe as fleshy lumps of meat. Blood dripped from the meat, staining the giant's hands as he leaned over the counter. He opened his hands with his palms facing up—a gesture of offering—and then extended them until they hovered over the box. With the giant's hands open, Buck had a good look at their contents.

He dry-heaved when he realized that the lumps of meat were two human hearts.

White smoke began to curl from the top of the Prexy box. The smoke was thin, floating in ribbons that resembled a woman's slender fingers. It grew denser as it climbed, surrounding the hearts and creating a cat's cradle over them. The giant held his position, though his hands were trembling. Wisps of black smoke rose from the two hearts. Buck blinked, wondering if he was hallucinating. Within the black smoke, he saw the profiles of two men, their mouths opened, screaming silently. The cat's cradle shrunk, encircling the profiles, trapping them in a vise built from the fingers of the white smoke. The profiles rose from the giant's hands, then floated down to the Prexy box, disappearing within it. It might have been Buck's imagination, but he thought the screams weren't so silent any more.

The pawnshop owner reached under the counter and Buck heard a short buzz. The owner nodded to the giant and said, "You can go now, Rex."

Turning to face Buck, the giant brought one of the hearts to his mouth. A pink tongue, thick, wide, and coated with spittle, jutted from his thick lips. Like a dog sampling road kill, the giant licked the heart. Buck's face tightened, and he looked away. After getting the expected reaction from Buck, the giant opened his mouth wide and slipped the heart between his lips. He clamped his teeth over his meal and inhaled. The giant chewed. Blood, as black as the giant's eyes, spurted from his mouth and over Buck's legs.

"That's enough, Rex. I told you to go!" The pawnshop owner sounded genuinely aggravated.

Staring hard at Buck, the giant put the remaining heart back into his pocket. He left without protest, walking toward the door he had originally used to enter the pawnshop. There was another buzzing sound, and the door slid closed. Buck turned his head back to the owner who was placing the Prexy box on the top shelf of the rack behind the counter. As he slipped a painting in front of the box, the pawnshop owner turned to Buck. "Please forgive Rex. He is without manners, but he is loyal."

The pawnshop owner walked around the counter and stood by Buck's side. "You have many questions I am sure, but you will not receive many answers. Though the fault is not yours, you have been pulled into a family conflict. Someone in my lineage currently resides in the Prexy box, and there are those who wish to release her. It would not be beneficial if she were to return." He paused in thought for a moment, and then went on. "I have said enough. Your involvement in our personal business is now over and you are free to go."

Instead of appearing grateful, Buck looked expectantly at the man.

"Your wife and daughter are unharmed."

Buck exhaled at the news and dropped his head. When he looked back up, the pawnshop owner continued.

"They were bound in one of the bedrooms. Except for what they heard, they have no knowledge of what took place. I'm afraid we left your home in quite a mess. You will have no choice but to call the authorities. I don't care what you tell them, but leave my involvement out of your story." The pawnshop owner then leaned forward until he was only inches from Buck's face. "Rex could have very easily transferred four souls to the Prexy Box."

Buck nodded. He understood the implication.

The pawnshop owner assisted him from the counter, supporting Buck as they walked to the front door and then through it. "For your sake, young man, I hope we never meet again." Buck said nothing as the man released him and went back into the shop.

The rain had not let up. Buck shambled out from the protection of the canopy, taking small uneasy steps toward the street. At the curb, he halted. Lifting his head, he let the rain wash over him.

It was time to go home.

"The Visitors" was written soon after I wrote "An Alabama Christmas". I felt so bad for Margaret in "An Alabama Christmas" that I wanted to write another story with a similar, older female character who didn't meet with a grisly end. But as my wife would say…the Devil got a hold of me. I failed miserably.

Two things come to mind about "The Visitors". The first is the reaction I got from the first readers when they came to the first twist. The story was written with the idea of leading readers on, to let them think they knew how the story would end early in the tale. When the first readers came to the twist, they stopped reading to email me. They let me know they were taken in. I'll never forget the feeling of accomplishment I had.

I also discovered with "The Visitors", the hardest part of writing a long story with only three characters comes with switching the points of view. It drove me nuts trying to come up with ways to credit characters in dialog or action without using their names over and over again.

I had sent "The Visitors" out only once for submission. It was rejected, though the editor enclosed a personal note to let me know he enjoyed the story and he had almost accepted it. His reason for rejecting it—I had used the same name over and over again to identify one of the characters. As is my custom, if a story is rejected once, I work on it and then put it in the trunk. I've made the changes I think the story deserves, and hope I figured them out to everyone's satisfaction.

THE VISITORS

Though unusual, but not entirely uncommon for an early October evening, fall announced its arrival at the Pine Cone Campground with a steep drop in temperature and blistering winds.

Broken tree limbs begetting broken glass, an endless sea of brightly colored leaves that would need raking, and a thin cover of ice over the pond—all further evidence that summer had finally pulled up stakes.

As proprietor of the Pine Cone Campground, Martha sighed at the inevitable end of camping season. Of course, the loss of revenue would be disappointing, but more to the point, Martha would miss the companionship of her customers. She genuinely enjoyed the camaraderie she shared with her seasonal regulars, not only receiving pleasure from their friendships but taking pride in their loyalty. She had always made it a point to socialize with the newer families that rented her cabins, often going out of her way to insure they were comfortable once they had arrived. Martha was, to put it simply, a people person.

The realization that another lonely winter wasn't all that far off weighed heavily on Martha. When her husband died seven years earlier, she had shut herself off from the rest of the world and devoted herself to running the campground. She never once considered starting a new romantic relationship. She thought herself too old, too frumpy, but more to the point, too simple for any man to desire her.

Lost in the thought of another Christmas spent alone, Martha walked behind the counter in the general store and approached the cash register. It was time to close up for the evening, a routine that she had no problem handling on autopilot. As she reached over to hit the cash-out button, she heard a noise so unexpected and intrusive that it jolted her from her thoughts.

It was as loud as the crack of a rifle and its echo reverberated throughout the building. The floor trembled for an instant, and Martha felt the vibration right through her canvas sneakers. A frightened whimper escaped her throat. She stepped back and lifted both of her arms, crossing them over her breasts.

Martha gasped as a cold wind slammed into her. It pushed her back as if it were solid, alive, attempting to pass right through her. Her cheeks stung from its bite and she shivered. Protecting her eyes, she narrowed them until they were small slits she could barely see through. Her gaze swept the interior of the store for the source, and when she discovered it, she was confused. At the front of the store, a large patch of darkness covered a section of the front wall. She opened her eyes wider, and though it took her a moment, she figured out what it was. Somehow, the oak door to the entrance of the general store had blown open and she was looking out into the darkness.

Peeved, Martha cursed and muttered something under her breath about it not being shut properly by the last customer. That loud crack she had heard must have been the wind taking that old, heavy door and slamming it against the inside wall. No wonder the building had shaken.

A metal display stand containing postcards and greeting cards that stood against the wall was missing, as was the small reading chair that was set next to it. Farther to her right, she saw them both toppled over, the chair on its side and the stand twisted—its racks empty.

The postcards and greeting cards, along with loose papers, foam cups, and anything else that hadn't been tied down, danced madly about in the air, supported by the gusts of wind billowing in through the open door. She worried that her face would be sliced open from the whirling debris, or even worse, that she would get hit with something heavier. With that last thought, she craned her neck and gazed on the shelves above her, scouring them for objects that could tumble off and fall.

This fear was short lived, replaced by another. Out of the corner of her eye, she spotted the silhouette of a young woman standing in the open doorway. Martha turned and watched as the young woman, clad only in jeans and a light T-shirt, inched her way across the threshold while maintaining a grip on the doorjamb. The young woman struggled against the wind's attempts to thrust her through the opening and into the display cases. The woman, feeling somewhat secure (either that, or she was exceeding brave, thought Martha), let go of the doorjamb. Martha watched as her visitor fumbled about trying to reach the door handle.

The young woman was not dressed appropriately for the weather and Martha noticed that she was thin and didn't have a lot of weight behind her. Martha thought that even if her visitor did manage to find the handle, it would be a struggle for her to close the door against the force of the wind.

Martha regained her composure, stooped and scurried behind the counter until she came to its end. She stayed low, battling her way against the wind to the front of the store. She slid as close to the wall as she could until she reached the door and then wedged herself behind it. Putting her own considerable weight against it, Martha and the young woman fought off the gales buffeting the store and managed to close the door. Inside, the blizzard of flying paper ceased, and all those airborne missiles drifted down to the floor.

Both women leaned their backs against the oak door and caught their breath. Martha used the time to look over her visitor and noticed her vibrant red, curly hair.

"Aren't you settled in cabin eight?" she asked, gasping. Martha was pretty sure she recognized the young woman from when she checked in.

"I am. Well…we are." the woman replied between her own deep breaths. "We were married last year, but with our business going so strong we never got a chance to get away. So we decided to take a couple of days off. We considered coming here a kind of late honeymoon."

"Well, what the hell are you doing out in this weather?" demanded Martha, her breath finally catching. "You can't need groceries that badly where you couldn't wait until morning! I was just going to close up the store. It's a good thing I was still here."

The two women pushed themselves from the door and walked toward the counter. "I had a fight with my husband," the young woman answered. "I know I shouldn't have gone out, but I was frustrated. I just couldn't get through to him. So I left and came here."

"If you don't mind my asking," Martha said in an even but still-peeved voice, "what were you two fighting about that made you risk a flight to the Land of Oz?"

"My name's Jane by the way," the young woman smiled sheepishly.

"Well, Jane, mine's Martha," the storekeeper replied while admiring the young woman's stunning blue eyes. "Now, what did you guys fight about?"

Jane bowed her head, and the trail of a single tear streaked down her cheek. "He wants to have a baby and I'm not ready, and..."

Jane's explanation was cut off with the sound of a loud bang. For the second time this evening, Martha was so startled that she thought she was going to jump out of her shoes. Then, in an encore performance, wind pummeled the inside of the store.

Both women turned toward the door and saw that it was wide open. Martha saw a large chunk of drywall on the floor. Then, in a moment that seemed all too surreal, Martha noticed another woman standing in the doorway, and this woman was just as poorly dressed for the weather as Jane was.

Martha thought this woman younger than herself but older than Jane. As for this woman's physique, she looked even thinner than Jane. A quick study of the woman's face indicated that she might be disoriented. Even more troubling, the woman was swaying so much in the doorway it looked as if at any moment the windstorm would declare victory in its apparent war with the store, and either fling her headlong into a display case or snatch her away.

Martha and Jane fought off the wind and approached the woman. When they reached her, each took hold of the woman's hands and led her inside. Once they were a safe distance from the door, Martha let go of the woman, made her way to the overturned chair, and returned with it. She and Jane seated the woman gently and for the second time that night, they both battled the wind to get the oak door closed.

After it was secured, Martha and Jane slowly made their way toward the woman, their chests hitching as they tried to catch their breath. As they neared, Martha saw the woman was shivering and offered her a coat. The woman said nothing and did not look up as the two hovered over her. Martha studied her and saw that the woman, like Jane, also had red hair, though it had faded to a dull, rusty color. Like Jane's, it was curly. Martha turned toward Jane and asked, "Is your mother staying with you?"

"No. I've never seen her before."

Martha was thoughtful for a second, and then addressed the woman. "I don't remember you checking in. Are you staying in the campground?"

In a somewhat raw voice, the woman replied while staring at her lap, "I've come a long distance to be here. I was here once, but it was a long time ago."

Martha looked at the woman with narrowed eyes. "I don't recall seeing you before. When were you here?

"I was here with my husband," the woman replied, ignoring the question. Without looking up she continued. "We were young and just married. We didn't have a honeymoon because I was so busy at work. So we decided to take a small break and spend the weekend here."

Her vocal cadence is odd, thought Martha. It was if she were reciting something from memory.

"Right after we arrived there was a windstorm," the woman went on, "which suited us just fine as we weren't planning on leaving the cabin anyway. But something went wrong. We had an argument."

Martha and Jane turned to look at one another, shock registering on their faces. Both turned back to the woman. With a hint of trepidation in her voice, Jane asked, "What…what happened?"

The woman looked up at Jane.

Martha immediately noticed her eyes. With a chill, she saw that they were a stunning bright blue. Just like Jane's. There was more than a passing facial resemblance between the two—the slant of her nose and the roundness of her jaw also reminded her of Jane. Once more, she thought that the woman could have been easily mistaken for Jane's mother. And she saw something else in the woman's eyes, something she struggled to place but couldn't put words to. Her eyes were cold, hard looking, and she wondered if the woman was concealing something.

Ignoring Martha, the woman continued to look deeply into Jane's eyes. Then, she answered Jane's question. "He wanted to have a baby and I didn't."

Jane gasped.

"I thought my career was more important," she continued, still speaking directly to Jane. "When he couldn't understand how I felt, I threw a book at him and I ran from the cabin. There was a terrible windstorm raging outside, but I was so mad at him I didn't want to go back."

At the mention of the windstorm, both Jane and Martha turned to look briefly at the front door of the store.

"I came here because I didn't know where else to go," the woman went on. "I wanted him to follow me, to chase me down...and make everything all right." The woman lowered her head before speaking again, this time her voice breaking, almost choking as she spoke. "Well, he did follow me. Halfway to the store the wind blew over a tree. He was right in its path. He was killed instantly."

Martha took her eyes off the woman and turned to look at Jane. *This can't be happening,* Martha thought. *It's impossible!* But everything was pointing to it: the blue eyes, the red hair, the similar facial features and, of course, their stories. Could this new visitor be an older Jane? Could these two be the same woman? How could this be possible? Martha kept moving her head back and forth between the two, trying to convince herself otherwise. But the more she compared the two women, the stronger the feeling grew.

Jane backed away from the woman, with her mouth open and her head shaking back and forth in disbelief. *In denial,* thought Martha. Then Jane paused and looked toward her. Jane brought her hand to her mouth, uttered a small cry, and then bolted toward the door. She was through it and out onto the dirt road before it had time to crash against the wall of the store.

Like a frequent guest that everyone abhorred, the wind roared back into the store and assaulted Martha and the woman. Cursing, Martha fought against the gusts as she walked to the doorway until she stood inside its frame. She held on tightly to the jamb on either side of her, and then looked out in the direction of cabin number eight. With her hair and clothes thrashing madly about her, she spread her legs wide until they also rested against the jambs, providing additional reinforcement against the wind's efforts to beat her back. Martha stood and waited. Seconds passed. Then, she heard it.

It was loud and powerful. She had no doubt as to its origin. The trunk of a tree had snapped. It was followed by a *thump* and the sound of wood splintering.

Sighing, Martha let go of the jamb, and with much effort managed to close the door. Exhausted, she walked to and stood above the woman, who remained seated. Gazing down at her, Martha replayed in her mind the series of events that had just occurred. As strange as everything seemed, she knew it wasn't a delusion. It had actually happened. She had witnessed it with her own eyes.

Martha found herself emotionally surrendering to the possibility of the situation and whispered softly to herself, "I hope she made it in time."

"I don't."

Martha reared her head back. Did she hear that right? "Excuse me?" she asked the woman. "What did you say?"

The woman gazed up at Martha, her face tight, her blue eyes brilliant and glaring. "I know what you are thinking," she said, her voice more alive now though somewhat condescending. "You think that I am her, that I came back to warn her about what was to happen and to prevent a tragedy. Well, you'd be partly right.

"Everything happened as I said it did. Her husband did die on this night. But what Jane didn't realize was that she was pregnant at the time. She discovered it shortly after the funeral, and once she was sure of it, she wanted to abort the child. But she couldn't bring herself to do it. She felt her husband's death was her fault, and the child was her penance. So a daughter was born. And Jane came to loath it.

"The demands of the child took a toll on her. She was unable to cope and she lost her job and all her career hopes. Jane was a rising executive, a star in her company, and she lost it all. She had no money. She became angry, bitter, and resentful of the child. She made her daughter's life a living hell. As soon as the child was able, she left her mother, but the damage was done. The child couldn't escape the hell she was brought up in. Her daughter turned to drugs to erase the memories of her mother's condemnations, and she prostituted herself to escape the loneliness. The stench of Jane's abuse lingered on the child for the rest of her life."

Martha was numb. Too many thoughts rushed through her mind and she had difficulty sorting them out.

Finally, after looking intently into the woman's face, realization broke through, and Martha spoke. "You're not her or her mother, are you? You're the child! Her child. And my God, you came back to save your father! You came back to warn Jane about the tree, so she could save his life. To make sure he was there to help raise you, and spare yourself the horrible life you led."

If the woman's eyes seemed brilliant earlier to Martha, she thought them ablaze now.

"No!" she shouted back at Martha. The woman stood up and leaned closer. Holding her arms out, she crossed her hands and grabbed at the hem of her shirt. She lifted it over her head and threw the shirt onto the floor. Martha gasped at the site.

She was braless and Martha saw a crisscross of old wounds scattered over her upper body. Almost every inch of her breasts and stomach was covered with scars. Most of the healed tissue consisted of crooked and jagged lines. Many of them looked like burns. The woman turned around and Martha saw similar markings on her back.

The woman faced Martha again, her eyes furious, and when she spoke, spittle flew from her lips. "She doesn't deserve to live, for what she did to me! She cut me, put lit cigarettes against my skin, and she would beat me until I was limp! She talked about this day constantly, drilling it into my head how unfair it was for her, as if it were my fault my father died! She reminded me every single damn day about how she was going to be rich, a famous business woman, and how I ruined everything for her! Can you imagine how it felt for me to be constantly reminded how useless I was? And how nobody would ever love me?"

The woman lowered her shoulders and her head dropped, the energy drained from her. She spoke again in a voice barely above a whisper. "And she was right; no one ever did love me. She made damned sure of that."

The woman looked at Martha, her face serious but with a hint of a smile. "I got a chance to come back. To make sure none of this would ever happen to me."

A gauntlet of emotions passed through Martha, all of them fighting for her attention at once, but she was too shocked to grab hold of even one of them and focus. Too much was happening and she couldn't put it into perspective. The whole scenario seemed like a nightmare she couldn't wake from. Then, as unbelievable as things had been already, something new happened that threatened to strain her grip on reality even more.

The woman faded before Martha's eyes.

"I lied when I told both of you my father died on the way here to the cabin." The woman spoke softly, her voice as thin as her form. The general store was bleeding through the woman, and Martha saw the fire in the woman's eyes was all but extinguished. A look of peace defined her features. The woman spoke one last time, her voice no louder than a whisper. "A tree fell on the cabin while he was still inside. He was crushed to death…there in the cabin. Not on the road."

She was gone.

Martha stood with her mouth agape, her body close to convulsing. She was unsure of what just happened. Her gaze focused on where the woman had stood, and then her eyes settled on the empty chair. Visions of the woman's abused body flashed in her mind, juxtaposed with an image of Jane. Martha had a difficult time conceiving that the lovely young newlywed was someone who would turn out to be so cruel later in life. Martha did the only thing she was capable of doing under the circumstances. She broke down sobbing.

After a time, when the tears dried up, she sat down onto the chair. She collected her thoughts.

Martha didn't know how long she sat there, but it took a while to put everything she had just experienced into some kind of order. Though she would never have all of her questions answered, she believed she understood enough to know what to do next. She rose from the chair, walked behind the counter, and grabbed her coat and cell phone.

The walk would be difficult in the wind, but Martha had no choice. She knew she had to go to cabin eight and to see for herself before she called 9-1-1. She was certain that after her trip to the cabin, she would be reporting the discovery of two dead campers.

Martha never expected the short walk to the door would be her last.

As Martha approached the door and reached for the knob, she was greeted with a blur of motion. Her first thought was that somehow the door had sprung to life. It rushed toward her like a tractor-trailer bearing down on a deer. With the force of the wind propelling it, the solid oak door slammed against her head. In an instant, Martha's view changed from that of the door to the general store's ceiling. Amid her surprise and confusion, she thought she had heard the sound of something snapping.

Martha laid on the floor stunned, her forehead throbbing. Worse, when she tried to lift herself, she couldn't move her body.

She remembered hearing that snapping sound.

Pain turned to fear when she thought she might be paralyzed. On the verge of panic, a figure appeared in her vision.

Jane looked down on her. The young woman's head was cocked to the side. One of her eyes was wide open and her lips were pursed.

Martha thought the door must have been left open as Jane's red hair was in constant motion, blowing around her face like tongues of flame celebrating a fire.

Despite her head pain, and the possibility of a more dire condition, Martha was relieved when she noticed that Jane had put on a light sweater and was better dressed for the weather.

"Jane," she said calmly, "I think I'm in trouble."

"I can see that."

"Please, call for some help."

Instead of reaching for a phone or leaving to get assistance, Jane continued to stand over Martha, studying the storekeeper's condition, as the wind whipped the contents of the general store around them. Then, without a word, she left Martha's side.

A minute later Jane reappeared, holding the chair that her daughter had been sitting in earlier. She lowered it next to Martha and sat down. Jane leaned over and stared at Martha.

"I don't know who that woman was, Martha, but she sure was crazy, huh?"

Shocked, Martha stared back at Jane. Could it be that Jane didn't understand what had happened? How could Jane not have made some kind of connection between herself and that woman?

Though Jane's eyes were peering deep into her own, Martha thought Jane was looking through her.

"You know, Martha," Jane continued, a smile creeping onto her lips, "I didn't tell you the whole truth about me."

Martha didn't reply. She had heard similar words spoken earlier, and she couldn't imagine Jane's confession being any less horrible than her daughter's.

"Yes, I did have a fight with my husband, that part was true. But what I didn't tell you was—just like that crazy woman did with her husband, before I left the cabin, I threw something at mine, too. Well, I guess I didn't really throw it at him. Actually, I came up behind him and smashed it against his head. It was a rock. And I hurt him bad, Martha. I killed him."

Jane's smile stretched a little wider.

"And yeah, I planned it before we got here, because, well, I lied to you about something else, too." Jane raised her eyebrows and frowned.

"I made it sound like we were two busy people who were working so hard we didn't have time for anything else. Well, the truth is, he worked packing boxes in a candy factory and I work as a sales clerk at the mall. But I have dreams, Martha! I've had them since I was a little girl. But, I know things are going to change and I'll be the one in charge. I'll be the one running the show one day." Jane beamed as she uttered the words.

"My husband was holding me back. He didn't believe in me. He loved me but he just couldn't give me the support I wanted or the money I needed to look like a business woman. What company would hire me if I was dressed like a housewife? Who would want me to run their business if I showed up to work in a beat-up old car? I knew the only way I could get that money was from his insurance. He said he was going to buy a lot of it because it was the smart way to save for a baby's future. Something about the cash value of the policy. I don't exactly understand it all, but I'm sure I will. He really wanted us to have a baby, to be a real family. I wasn't lying when I said I wasn't ready for a baby. It would have interfered with my plans. I'm going to take that insurance money and start a new life."

Martha's eyes went to Jane's stomach.

"I know what you're thinking, Martha," Jane chuckled. "You

think that maybe someday, I will have a baby, and maybe you're right, but I just couldn't have one now. And you know, when I do have a baby, I hope it's a girl. I'm going to tell her how successful I was, how I worked hard to climb my way to the top. Every single day I'm going to remind that little girl how fortunate she is to be my daughter." Then Jane added, "I'm going to give her the most wondrous life possible. I am going to love that little girl to death, Martha." Jane paused and her eyes lost focus.

Martha thought that Jane might be imagining what her life would be like with a daughter. If she had any feeling below her neck, she would have felt her own stomach clenching. She knew that Jane was pregnant right now, and Martha's thoughts turned to the tortuous life that lay ahead for the baby.

"Well, where was I?" asked Jane, snapping out whatever delusional scenes had been playing in her head. "Oh yeah…after that woman came in here earlier with that crazy story, I thought that she might have somehow discovered my husband in the cabin and was trying to get me to admit to killing him. When I got back to the cabin, I saw that the door was still locked and the curtains were all closed, so there was no way she could have known what I did. I went inside to check, too, just in case. She was just a crazy woman, don't you think? By the way, where is she?"

Martha didn't know how to respond so she remained silent. Jane didn't seem to notice.

"I really owe her a debt of gratitude. She gave me an idea on how to explain my husband's death. I just dragged him out of the cabin and put him next to one of the bigger trees that were blown over. And you're not going to believe this, Martha, but after I got him out, another huge tree blew over and landed right on our cabin!" With her rump still firmly planted in the chair, Jane bent over until her face was only inches above Martha's.

With the wind blowing at her back, Jane's hair continued to fly wildly about. Then, her eyes widened, and with an almost childlike expression of sincerity on her face, Jane nodded her head slowly and added, "I could have been inside that cabin with him and we'd both be dead."

Martha groaned. It was all for nothing, she thought. Her daughter came back to prevent all of this from happening but it didn't work. She wondered how Jane's daughter reacted when she found herself back where she came from, not only alive, but in the same circumstances as she was before her trip.

As for Martha, she was faring no better, instead worse. Here she was, lying on her back, unable to move her body, and with a deranged killer staring her in the face. She had never been more helpless in her life.

"Please," Martha whispered, pleading to Jane, "The door, it hit me in the head. I—I can't move. Please, help me!"

A look of concern crossed Jane's face and she stood from the chair. With debris flying around her, Jane moved toward the counter and was out of Martha's view for a moment. When she returned, she stood out of Martha's sight.

"Did you feel that?" Jane asked from somewhere near.

"No," Martha whispered back.

"How about that?"

"No."

Jane floated into Martha's view and sat back down in the chair. "I kicked you twice Martha, once in the leg and once in the side. You said you didn't feel either of the kicks. I think you're paralyzed."

"I'm going to help you, Martha. Being paralyzed is no way to spend the rest of your life." Jane rose from the chair.

She straddled Martha's head, bent her legs and lowered herself until her knees made contact with the floor. She then lowered her rump until it hovered within an inch of Martha's chest. Jane let her full weight fall onto Martha.

Martha's reaction was immediate. Her mouth ballooned wide and her lips violently parted as the air from her lungs was forced through her windpipe. Martha's head lifted rapidly from the floor, and her eyes bulged from the pressure. Moments later, when all the air from her chest was expelled, Martha's head slammed back down. Black spots swam in her vision.

Jane giggled at the sight. She wiggled her rump, pretending to adjust herself on Martha's breasts in order to make herself more comfortable. Then, she sat quietly, and with one eye half closed, she tilted her head slightly and studied Martha.

There was nothing Martha could do but stare up at Jane. Her crazy visitor's hair continued its mad dance about her head. Martha hoped to find a hint of compassion in Jane's eyes, maybe even hear a few words of sympathy. Instead, she was met with indifference. As Jane stared at her, Martha had the impression that Jane was memorizing every wrinkle, vein, and pockmark on her face. She was about to speak, to beg Jane for help, but Jane's eyes had become slightly vacant. Could a memory have intruded into Jane's thoughts? Was Jane mulling something over?

As if answering a question Martha had never asked out loud, Jane nodded and grinned. Then, Jane's left hand rose. Martha followed it with her eyes until it disappeared behind Jane's back. Seconds later, Jane's hand returned clutching something. She lowered her closed fist in front of Martha's face. Like an owner teasing a dog with a treat, Jane waved her fist back and forth. Martha followed along, but the strain on her eyes proved to be too much, and she focused back on Jane's face. Tiring of the game, Jane stopped, turned her hand over, and opened her fingers so Martha could see what she was holding.

It was a small utility knife.

Grinning, Jane thumbed the slide on top of the knife forward, extending the blade until it could go no further. Martha thought Jane must have taken it from the counter, right before she had kicked her.

In her peripheral vision, Martha caught Jane's other hand as it moved slowly toward her until Martha's view consisted of nothing but the lines and creases on Jane's palm and fingers.

Spreading her fingers slightly, Jane pushed them against Martha's forehead until she couldn't move her head. Terrified, she could only watch what happened between the spaces of Jane's fingers.

Jane lowered the utility knife gently to the side of Martha's head, resting it against her neck, and then Martha caught a quick motion out of the corner of her eye. Jane's upper body had jerked. Martha attempted to scream, but with Jane's hand over her mouth the sound was muffled.

Jane had just sliced open her neck.

Leaning forward, Jane inspected her handiwork. Satisfied as to its effectiveness, she removed her hand from Martha's face and leaned back. With a smile etched on her face, she watched and waited for Martha to die.

Though Martha could not feel its dampness, she could imagine the blood pooling around her body, the puddles forming dark, thick, and slow-moving streams as it followed along the seams in the floorboards. It was only a matter of time before she bled to death. She thought she could already feel herself growing sleepy.

As her pulse waned and she waited for the darkness to envelope her, Martha's eyes wandered back up to Jane's. Once again she was struck by their intensity. Martha had no doubt that Jane was insane. She replayed the day's events in her head, wondering how she had offended God so much that he would let her die like this. While recounting her conversation with Jane's daughter, something the poor woman had said earlier came back to Martha.

"She had no money."

Martha had always put others before herself, so it was not surprising that her last thoughts were not of her own impending death but of the woman who was killing her. She thought Jane was not only insane but stupid. Jane should have made certain that her husband had gotten around to purchasing all that insurance he was talking about before she punched that rock against his head.

If she was going to die at the hands of this crazy woman, Martha was determined to make her final moments count for something. Though it might be the last thing she would ever see, Martha was now burning with desire to see the expression on Jane's face when she learned that her plan had failed. Jane may have gotten away with murdering her husband, but due to her half-assed planning, she would wind up penniless.

Martha struggled for the strength to share her revelation with Jane, but she was too weak to speak. Instead, she did the only thing she had strength enough to do. Martha simply smiled into the face of her murderer.

The smile on Jane's face straightened.

Martha wished she could read Jane's thoughts.

Jane's expression turned blank, as if she had gone into a trance.

Martha imagined that the gears turning inside of Jane's head had slipped, that they were off track now, her mind slowing to a crawl—maybe an all-out stop. Could Jane have realized that there was something wrong, terribly wrong, and she was having a difficult time processing it?

As quickly as the question entered her mind, Martha knew she was mistaken. Jane's face stiffened, and her eyes narrowed.

The wind echoed Jane's change. The gusts through the open door increased in pitch, and the wind was now strong enough to move heavier objects that hadn't budged earlier. A wooden barrel filled with apples toppled over and the fruit rushed toward her, the Macintoshes rolling past her as easily as tumbleweeds.

The increase of the wind's howling hurt Martha's ears, but above the noise, she could hear another sound. She couldn't place it at first but then she recognized it—the sound of wood snapping. The store was falling apart around her. As important as the building was in her lifetime, its fate had little effect on her, though she did wonder if she would remain alive long enough to see the extent of the damage. She returned her focus to Jane and an image of Medusa, with her snake-infested head and wild, glassy eyes, popped into Martha's head.

With a motion so quick that Martha had little time to register it, Jane raised her arms over her head. Uttering a cry of fury, Jane brought the knife down, the point aimed at Martha's left eye. Martha tracked its descent without fear. She closed her eyes, and waited for the tip of the blade to strike.

There was no pain. Instead, Martha heard the *thunk* of the knife's tip as it buried itself into the floor, next to her left ear. Her eyes opened at the sound.

Jane was still sitting on her chest but she was leaning forward, her face only a foot away from Martha's. Jane's eyes were glazed, wide, and showed no sign of life. Her lower jaw hung and her cheeks were sunken. Her lips were open but frozen in place, as if the last word she had uttered was, "*oh*."

A large piece of wood jutted from between Jane's breasts.

Martha stared at the tip of the stake. Long, freshly torn bits of flesh had caught on the wood as it had traveled through Jane's body. Struggling against the wind, a steady stream of blood dripped. The blood never made it onto Martha's chest as the wind snatched it away as soon as it lost contact with the wood. The wood stuck out around six inches from Jane, and the tip was angled toward Martha's chest.

Martha understood enough of what had happened to summon a weak smile of gratitude. She wondered if Jane's daughter had returned somehow to finish the job. Weakly, Martha turned her head to look around for her, and then realized that Jane's daughter had nothing to do with her mother's death. The roof of the store had collapsed. Uneven piles of broken wood and torn shingles were strewn everywhere. No, Jane had nothing to do with this.

Martha wasn't sure if it was a strong gust of wind or if another piece of the roof had fallen, but she wasn't prepared when Jane's body suddenly pitched forward. Jane's forehead collided with hers. Though she couldn't feel it, Martha knew with certainty that the end of the wooden stake had just punctured her chest.

Blood, darkly hued and mixed with tissue, spouted from Martha's mouth. It bubbled about her lips and flowed down her chin. She choked from the reservoir pooling in her mouth. The exertion caused bright stars to swim before her eyes, even as her vision darkened. Before the blackness claimed her completely, she felt a presence close by. She turned her head to look. More blood spilled from her mouth and onto the floor, enlarging a puddle she imagined was already bigger than she was.

Martha didn't have much time to process her last vision.

She saw Jane's daughter.

The young woman gazed down upon Martha. The wind that had wreaked so much havoc this evening had stilled, and the blackness that had come to claim Martha appeared to retreat in deference to her visitor. The young woman was naked—her skin smooth, devoid of the burns and scars that had once desecrated her body. She was only there for a moment. Jane's daughter faded from Martha's view.

Martha's thoughts were jumbled, but there was one that stood out amid the clutter. If Jane was dead, how could her daughter come back?

Before Martha exhaled her last breath, an image of her husband drifted into her mind, a sign. She hoped that there would be no more Christmases spent alone.

ABOUT THE AUTHOR

Tony Tremblay is a horror fiction writer who has published a number of short stories and nonfiction. He is also the host of *The Taco Society Presents*, a horror-themed talk show on G-TV based out of Goffstown, N.H. (it can be also be viewed on YouTube). Tony is a reviewer of genre-based fiction and had reviewed for *Horror World*, *Cemetery Dance Magazine*, and *Beware The Dark Magazine*. He lives in New Hampshire with his wife Paula.

Curious about other Crossroad Press books?
Stop by our site:
http://store.crossroadpress.com
We offer quality writing
in digital, audio, and print formats.

Enter the code FIRSTBOOK
to get 20% off your first order from our store!
Stop by today!

CPSIA information can be obtained at www.ICGtesting.com
Printed in the USA
BVOW06s1157060516

447015BV00003B/7/P

9 781941 408780